Simply Learning, Simply Best!

Simply Learning, Simply Best!

倍斯特出版事業有限公司
Best Publishing Ltd.

新制多益
聽力題庫

短獨白❷ (附詳盡解析)

TOEIC

Amanda
Chou◎ 著

四大特色

1 聽、讀雙效強化：**包含聽力和閱讀獨家學習設計**
　巧妙運用聽和讀之間的關聯性，演練聽力亦同步強化閱讀，一石二鳥攻略新制多益聽力+閱讀。

2 循環必考字彙演練：**神助攻字彙記憶學習**
　精選各大類考試必考字彙並融入短獨白中，達到舉一反三和速記字彙的功效。

3 關鍵翻譯和句型納入：**同步提升英語說、寫能力**
　收錄千句膾炙人口、即學即用的表達句，口說、寫作和翻譯等課程高分唾手可得。

4 美劇道地用語強化：**培養具備無字幕觀看的實力**
　具備無字幕觀看能力（同於考場中僅能仰賴耳朵聽），「耳到」後聽力迅速高分。

MP3

作者序

　　在新多益聽力測驗，英文短獨白的題目佔了總題數的30%，卻包含了各類型式的聽力表達內容，例如：新聞報導、超市公告、談話和廣告等等（在《短獨白(1)》 Part 2中收錄的主題是比較基礎型的新多益短獨白題型），也涵蓋了較進階的主題，像是Part 3實境直播的叢林探險、水族館、藝廊和慈善會。這些主題繼續延伸的話就成了在Part 1中收錄的胡椒蝦等特定專業主題，難度也較為高些。重點是，這樣的規劃更能強化學習者的整合能力，除了聽力面向的強化。畢竟，能夠運用聽、說、讀和寫之間巧妙關係的學習者，能以更短的時間和路徑達到學習成效。

　　在《短獨白(2)》，也延續了《短獨白(1)》的規劃，除了強化新多益聽力中短獨白的答題能力外，也能潛移默化中記憶在各類考試，例如：新多益聽力和閱讀、學測和指考中常考的字彙、提升答新多益閱讀字彙、文法、短文填空、學測指考中字彙、綜合測驗、文意選填和篇章結構等的答題能力。除此之外，也能修正介係詞等的使用和大幅提升口說和翻譯能力。考生在反覆聽誦後可以從三個PART當中掌握關鍵字彙、道地慣用語、各類句型、答題語感、聽力專注力等，一次性提升整合英語實力。

如果是剛升高一的考生更可以利用這兩本書的練習彌補掉國三升高一時面對英語學習的吃力感。（在基測、特招等英語都考取滿分的考生或分數相同的考生，到高中時卻差異日益漸大，到高三考學測指考時分數差距更為顯著，當然還包含了很多其他因素。）若能持之以恆的使用書中的單元，於每天或每週定期的練習（也可於通勤和下課時聽誦），相信效果會等同於每天固定練習一定題數的數學題的學習者一樣，最終在各個英語考試中都能獲取佳績，並能提升自己未來求職競爭力。

Amanda Chou

使用說明

INSTRUCTIONS

UNIT ❸

金門貢糖和高粱酒

▶ 影子跟讀「短獨白」練習　🎧 MP3 003

此篇為「影子跟讀短獨白練習」，規劃了由聽「短獨白」的shad-owing練習，強化聽力專注力和掌握各個考點，現在就一起動身，開始聽「短獨白」！

Kinmen is a popular tourist destination that is known for quaint architecture and beaches. There are two specialty items a tourist should look for. The first is Kimen Peanut Candy. Many stores sell the peanut candy and most will encourage the buyer to try it before buying. However, buying the candy from a store that weighs it will give you more candy for the same price as the pre-boxed kind.

金門是一個有名的觀光景點，以古色古香的建築及其美麗的海灘而著稱。這裡有兩個旅客必看的項目。第一是金門貢糖。在金門街上有很多賣貢糖的店，很多店家也都會有試吃再買的服務，秤斤的貢糖會比較划算，秤斤與盒裝數量會差到少二倍。

The second item is Kinmen Kaoliang Liquor which has a rich fragrance and is strong tasting. When compared to popular Taiwan alcohol, such as rice wine, wine, beer, and Shaoxing wine, the Kinmen Kaoliang Liquor has a higher alcohol concentration. Liquor in White Urn (with a 58.38 % alcoholic concentration) can only be bought in Kinmen. Warning: there are still mines in Kinmen. Although the mined area has signs, tourists still need to be careful and not mistakenly step on one!

再來是金門的高粱酒，因為氣候的關係以高粱釀出的酒醣育出芬芳氣味和濃郁口味，對於酒外行的遊客來説，到金門買高粱酒要注意的是，比起一般在臺灣普遍的米酒，葡萄酒，啤酒和紹興酒來説，酒精濃度高很多，像是只能在金門買到的白色甕裝，含有濃度 58%的酒精。金門的太陽很強烈，出門一定要注意防曬，另外要注意的就是金門現在還是有很多的地雷，雖然地雷區都會有標示，但是還是小心不要誤踩！

1　短獨白「影子跟讀」和填空測驗
2　短語在精準論述計時
3　短篇口譯短誦測驗

涵蓋各豐富主題
鞏固基礎實力
道地表達句強化翻譯、口譯等英語能力

· 藉由零碎時間反覆聽誦，無形中便能回想到主題中的字句、甚至隨著時間，更能朗朗上口，猶如勢如破竹般的提升口説、翻譯和口譯實力。

「影子跟讀」強化聽力耳
聽力專注力立馬到位，答題不失分

· 由「中英對照」的對話以影子跟讀法進行練習，從「看原稿跟著音檔讀」逐步延伸至「只播放音檔也能同步跟著讀」等等的練習，打好聽力專注力基礎。並於具備一定的聽力專注力後再輔以海量的試題搭配練習，分數迅速狂飆。

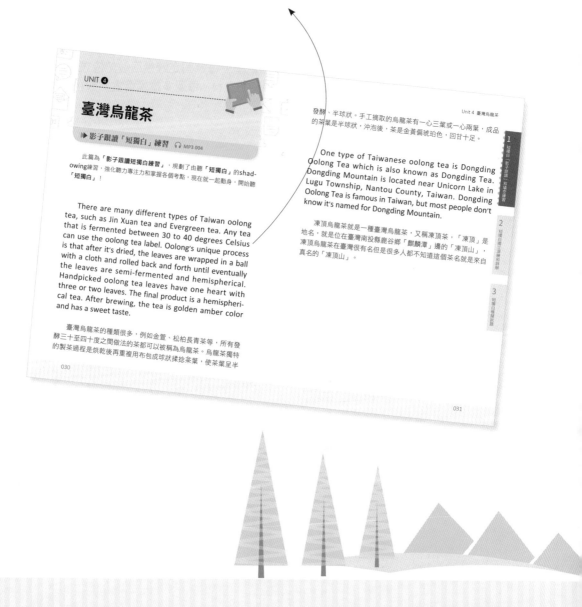

UNIT ❹

臺灣烏龍茶

▶ 影子跟讀「短獨白」練習　🎧 MP3 004

此篇為「影子跟讀短獨白練習」，規劃了由聽「短獨白」的shadowing練習，強化聽力專注力和掌握各個考點，現在就一起動身，開始聽「短獨白」！

There are many different types of Taiwan oolong tea, such as Jin Xuan tea and Evergreen tea. Any tea that is fermented between 30 to 40 degrees Celsius can use the oolong tea label. Oolong's unique process is that after it's dried, the leaves are wrapped in a ball with a cloth and rolled back and forth until eventually the leaves are semi-fermented and hemispherical. Handpicked oolong tea leaves have one heart with three or two leaves. The final product is a hemispherical tea. After brewing, the tea is golden amber color and has a sweet taste.

臺灣烏龍茶的種類很多，例如金萱、松柏長青茶等，所有發酵三十至四十度之間做法的茶都可以被稱為烏龍茶。烏龍茶獨特的製茶過程是烘乾後再重複用布包成球狀揉捻茶葉，使茶葉呈半

030

發酵、半球狀。手工摘取的烏龍茶有一心三葉或一心兩葉，成品的茶葉是半球狀，沖泡後，茶是金黃偏琥珀色，回甘十足。

Unit 4 臺灣烏龍茶

One type of Taiwanese oolong tea is Dongding Oolong Tea which is also known as Dongding Tea. Dongding Mountain is located near Unicorn Lake in Lugu Township, Nantou County, Taiwan. Dongding Oolong Tea is famous in Taiwan, but most people don't know it's named for Dongding Mountain.

凍頂烏龍茶就是一種臺灣烏龍茶，又稱凍頂茶，「凍頂」是地名，就是位在臺灣南投縣鹿谷鄉「麒麟潭」邊的「凍頂山」，凍頂烏龍茶在臺灣很有名但是很多人都不知道這個茶名就是來自真名的「凍頂山」。

1　短獨白「影子跟讀」和試題練習題

2　短獨白填空補充資料

3　短獨白試題練習題

031

教師的最佳幫手、學生的最佳助力
破解各類型英語測驗的出題
掌握關鍵字彙和語法

· 藉由聽力填空練習，同步修正口語表達、各類型英語考試中的詞類挖空、強化各主題的字彙能力，內建超強語感，迅速獲取高分。

· 學生可於高一即開始每周練習數個單元，並反覆聽誦，升高三時輕鬆對戰學測、指考綜合測驗等題型。

· 教師可於每堂英語課開頭花數分鐘測驗學生某單元的填空練習，或指定學生每週固定練幾回並記憶該篇所有字彙（效果等同於國文科，每週多讀幾篇古文觀止選文）。

UNIT **9**

買咖啡體驗

▶ 影子跟讀「短獨白填空」練習　⏵ MP3 009

除了前面的「**影子跟讀短獨白練習**」，現在試著在聽著對話後，完成下列填空練習，從中強化生活場景中常見的字彙以及拼字能力，答案的話請參照前面的獨白！

In Taiwan, you can buy _____ coffee every-where - at _____ stores and at the _____ coffee chain stores. These highly _____ shops not only serve cheap coffee, but most _____ the coffee fresh and are _____ about the _____ of the coffee fee. Their goal is to serve inexpensive high _____ coffee quickly. Some of the bigger coffee shops have coffee roasting machines, while other _____ sell a _____ variety of coffee making _____ to use at _____.

在臺灣到處都可以買到平價咖啡，便利商店和大型咖啡連鎖店都可以買到平價咖啡。這些有名的店不僅賣便宜的咖啡，很多是現磨現煮，也都非常注重品質。他們的目標就是要賣快速高品質的平價咖啡。有大型的店還會擺設咖啡烘焙機，也會賣一些可

以家庭用的泡咖啡器具。

Unit 9 買咖啡體驗

However, the best thing to do is to go _____ and find the small coffee shops in the _____ and _____ of the big cities. This type of coffee shop is _____ quite small, and the _____ of the coffee shop _____ the owner's _____. Coffee _____ share their experiences with the small coffee shops in _____ and in the _____ online, making it _____ for tourists to find the _____ cup of coffee.

其實如果你有閒情逸致的話，很多大城市裡不起眼的小巷弄裡會有很多有特色的咖啡店，這類型的特色都是小小的，但通常會表現出老闆自己品味的特色。網路上很容易找到這樣的資料，很多個人部落格裡也會分享自己對這些巷弄裡的咖啡店的經驗。咖啡愛好者會在部格格分享他們在小咖啡店的經驗，也會在網路寫評論，這些資料可以讓遊客很方便的尋找一杯完美的咖啡。

Unit 3
動物園公告：鱷魚上演了大逃亡，但講者顯然把重點放在別地方了XDD

🎙 Instructions

❶ 請播放音檔聽下列對話，並完成試題。 🎧 MP3 051

77. Why does the speaker say, "Oops...My office glass wall just shattered"?
(A) The glass was not bulletproof.
(B) The glass was shot by bullets.
(C) The police officers shot the glass.
(D) The glass was destroyed by the crocodiles.

78. What are the visitors told to do when they see the crocodiles?
(A) start panicking.
(B) remain calm.
(C) call the police.
(D) call animal specialists.

79. How is the weather on the day of this announcement?
(A) very hot
(B) warm
(C) very cold
(D) cool

聽力原文和對話

Questions 77-79 refer to the following announcement

Attention visitors! I do hope you enjoy your day in the zoo, and I'm here to inform you that our crocodiles seem to decide to have a day off or something. They're not in their compartments. But it's chilly out there. I'm not sure why they have to take a weekend getaway or something. I don't want you guys to panic. I've four animal specialists and police officers out there looking for them already. When you see them, just to keep calm...and you'll be fine...OMG what are they doing out there. Oops...My office glass wall just shattered. Apparently, I was fooled by Glass Company. It can't stand crocodile's punch.

問題77-79請參閱下列公告

觀光者們注意！我希望你們都能享受在動物園的時光，我在此是要告知你們我們的鱷魚們似乎決定想休息一天或幹嘛的。他們不在我們的隔間裡。但是外頭相當寒冷。我不知道為什麼他們想要上演個周末大逃亡或什麼的。我不想要你們感到驚嚇。我已經派四個動物專人和警察們找尋他們。當你們看到他們就保持冷靜...我想你們會沒事的...天啊他們在這幹嘛...糟了...我的辦公司玻璃剛剛碎掉了。顯然我被玻璃公司騙了。它無法承受鱷魚的撞擊。

答案： 77. D 78. B 79. C

多軌強化聽力，學習一次到位！
【試題＋影子跟讀＋解析】

· 試題演練後，隨即對照解析觀看，並反覆利用聽力原文進行「影子跟讀」演練，多重強化聽力練習。

出。）

選項中譯和解析

77. 為何講者說「糟了...我的辦公司玻璃牆剛碎掉了」？
　(A) 玻璃牆不防彈。
　(B) 玻璃牆被子彈射擊。
　(C) 警官射擊玻璃牆。
　(D) 玻璃牆被鱷魚破壞了。

78. 訪客被告知看到鱷魚時該做什麼？
　(A) 開始驚慌。
　(B) 保持鎮定。
　(C) 打電話給警察。
　(D) 打電話給動物專家。

79. 在此宣布當天天氣如何？
　(A) 很熱。
　(B) 溫暖。
　(C) 很冷。
　(D) 涼爽。

77.
・這題也是較具鑑別度的一題，要聽懂"Oops...My office glass wall just shattered"。綜合短講開頭描述「鱷魚們......不在我們的隔間裡」（our crocodiles ...... They're not in their compartments.）及考點的句子的上一句:OMG what are they doing out there.，推測they指的是鱷魚，因此玻璃牆剛碎掉和鱷魚關係最密切，**故選(D)**。（還要注意的是，這是這個題組的短獨白末的訊息，但是卻擺在這個題組的第一題。）

78.
・這題也是要小心的一題，根據When you see them, just to keep calm，知道講者告訴訪客保持鎮定。**故選(B)**。（但有些時候，卻因為很仔細聽講者的表達和情緒起伏，在選的時候讓誤選了其他選項，要注意區分「剛才有聽到講者說過」和「是否是題目所問的」。）

79.
・此細節題詢問天氣，根據But it's chilly out there.，chilly，形容詞，寒冷的，**故選(C)**。（這題是剛開頭提到到快中段時的訊息，但卻擺在這個題組最後一題出，還有要注意的是，別憑感覺答題。）

附選項中譯和詳盡解析
徹底理解所有出題脈絡

・提供更多元的答題思路，逐步協助考生進行推論或刪去誘答選項，釐清頭緒後迅速判答，如同有英文家教在旁的神力加持，自關自學即可完成所有試題並具備應考判答實力。

演練 10 篇為一組的英文短獨白
適應應考時英文對話節奏

· 習慣性聽此長度的英文短獨白，立即熟悉一整回聽力模擬試題中短獨白的練習量（即 10 篇），漸進式養成具備獨立撰寫聽力試題的實力。

· 搭配所附的中英對照和解析，雙重檢視學習成果，一舉攻略新多益聽力。

聽力模擬試題

▶ PART 4 🎧 MP3 059

Directions: In this part, you will listen to several talks by one or two speakers. These talks will not be printed and will only be spoken one time. For each talk, you will be asked to answer three questions. Select the best response and mark the corresponding letter (A), (B), (C), (D) on your answer sheet.

71. Why does the man say, "a bit overshadowed by"?
(A) because he exaggerates the claim
(B) because he wants the flagstone as a gift from villagers
(C) because he thinks the flagstone actually prevails the company's expensive products
(D) because now he cannot cook faster

72. Why does the man want the camera to have a close-up?
(A) to make villagers jealous
(B) to impress the producer of the show
(C) to give photographers a genuine feel
(D) to highlight and promote the product

73. What distinguishes the food processor with villagers' knife?
(A) its engine
(B) its efficiency
(C) its price
(D) its weight

74. What is being advertised?
(A) the Chinese woks
(B) the dough with scallions
(C) fried water spinach
(D) the ladle

75. What aspect of the pan does the speaker applaud?
(A) the origin
(B) the light weight
(C) the heating part
(D) the shipment

76. Who most likely is the speaker addressing?
(A) housewives
(B) villagers
(C) executives of the kitchen wares
(D) the producer

77. What can be inferred about the merger?
(A) successful
(B) fruitful
(C) futile
(D) mysterious

78. Which of the following is closest in meaning to disintegrate?
(A) intact
(B) mystify
(C) consolidate
(D) dismiss

79. Why does the spokesperson say, "adds salt to injury"?
(A) To salvage the public image of the company
(B) to provide proof of the transferred money
(C) to refute the information from earlier news report

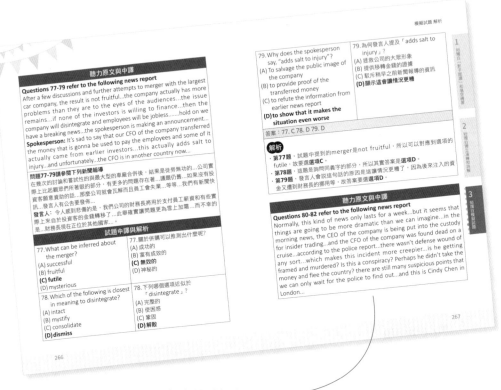

聽力原文與中譯

Questions 77-79 refer to the following news report
After a few discussions and further attempts to merger with the largest car company, the result is not fruitful...the company actually has more problems than they are to the eyes of the audiences...the issue remains...if none of the investors is willing to finance...then the company will disintegrate and employees will be jobless.......hold on we have a breaking news...the spokesperson is making an announcement...
Spokesperson: It's sad to say that our CFO of the company transferred the money that is gonna be used to pay the employees and some of it actually came from earlier investors...this actually adds salt to injury...and unfortunately...the CFO is in another country now...

問題77-79請參閱下列新聞報導
在幾次的討論和嘗試性的與最大型的車廠合併後，結果是徒勞無功的...公司實際上比起觀眾們所著眼的部分，有更多的問題存在著...議題仍舊...如果沒有投資者願意資貸的話...那麼公司就會瓦解而且員工會失業...等等...我們有新聞快訊...發言人有公告要發佈...
發言人： 令人感到悲傷的是，我們公司的財務長將用於支付員工薪資和有些實際上來自於投資客的金錢轉移了...此舉確實讓傷口要雪上加鹽...而不幸的是...財務長現在正位於其他國家...。

試題中譯與解析

77. What can be inferred about the merger?	77. 關於併購可以推測出什麼呢？
(A) successful	(A) 成功的
(B) fruitful	(B) 富有成效的
(C) futile	**(C) 無效的**
(D) mysterious	(D) 神秘的
78. Which of the following is closest in meaning to disintegrate?	78. 下列哪個選項近似於「disintegrate」？
(A) intact	(A) 完整的
(B) mystify	(B) 使困惑
(C) consolidate	(C) 鞏固
(d) dismiss	**(D) 解散**

79. Why does the spokesperson say, "adds salt to injury"?
(A) To salvage the public image of the company
(B) to provide proof of the transferred money
(C) to refute the information from earlier news report
(D) to show that it makes the situation even worse

79. 為何發言人提及「adds salt to injury」？
(A) 拯救公司的大眾形象
(B) 提供移轉金錢的證據
(C) 駁斥稍早之前新聞報導的資訊
(D) 顯示這會讓情況更糟

答案：77. C 78. D 79. D

解析
- 第77題，試題中提到的merger是not fruitful，所以可以可以對應到選項的futile，故要選選項D。
- 第78題，這是詢問同義字的部分，所以其實答案是選項D。
- 第79題，發言人會說這句話的原因是這讓情況更糟了，因為後來注入的資金又遭到財務長的挪用等，故答案要選選項D。

聽力原文與中譯

Questions 80-82 refer to the following news report
Normally, this kind of news only lasts for a week...but it seems that things are going to be more dramatic than we can imagine...in the morning news, the CEO of the company was found dead on a cruise...according to the police report...there wasn't defense wound of any sort...which makes this incident more creepier...is he getting framed and murdered? Is this a conspiracy? Perhaps he didn't take the money and flee the country? there are still many suspicious points that we can only wait for the police to find out...and this is Cindy Chen in London...

強化整合答題能力
無懼任何出題陷阱和「結合數個聽力訊息考點」的出題迅速拆解各式題型

- 包含❶將聽到的訊息轉換成「形容詞」的同義轉換❷要「理解慣用語」才能選對的試題❸需要綜合訊息後才理解的新聞類話題❹包含「較為進階」的計算❺在所提供的聽力訊息有限的情況下，要搭配「刪去法」的答題❻部分要理解某些「進階字彙」才能答的試題❼區別近似或重疊性的聽力訊息，且容易誤選的試題，詳細釐清題目到底問什麼等等。

目次
CONTENTS

Part 2　短獨白獨立演練和詳解

Part 3 短獨白模擬試題

· 【叢林探險(1)：廚具】高級烹飪廚具跟村民的石板相比似乎有
點相形見絀

- 【叢林探險(2)：廚具】居民的木製長柄勺也太好
- 【倍斯特汽車大廠(1)】財務長捲款而逃
- 【倍斯特汽車大廠(2)】執行長因為涉及內線交易而被拘留
- 【消防局】倉庫爆炸和大型的森林火災...所幸出現奇蹟
- 【倍斯特珠寶展(1)】一票難求的珠寶展,有四種類型的珠寶
- 【倍斯特珠寶展(2)】新聞發佈到現在,終於見到「珠寶問世」
- 【下午新聞播報】颱風的三個路徑預測,其中一個預測和國際新聞預測吻
- 【倍斯特博物館】數以千計的觀光客都會跟活現的火山和湖泊形成的模型拍照
- 【倍斯特電視】價值連城的城堡主人來電視節目中參加通告

- 收錄琳琅滿目的主題，除了基礎的核心能力強化外，考生更能從書中的各主題段落強化各種句型表達，在口說、口譯和翻譯能力都能有顯著的成效，一次搞定所有大小考試且令周遭人感到驚艷。

Part

1

短獨白「影子跟讀」
和填空練習

UNIT ❶

台灣夜市小吃

▶▶ **影子跟讀「短獨白」練習** 🎧 MP3 001

此篇為「影子跟讀短獨白練習」，規劃了由聽「短獨白」的shadowing練習，強化聽力專注力和掌握各個考點，現在就一起動身，開始聽「短獨白」！

You can't visit Taiwan without visiting a night market. Many tourists' favorite place is not the National Palace Museum or the CKS Memorial Hall, but the night market. There are 319 towns in Taiwan, each with their own version of the night market (large and small). Each night market reflects the unique culture and food of the area.

你如果沒逛過夜市，就不能說你有來過臺灣，很多外國遊客最喜歡臺灣的地方不是故宮博物院或中正紀念堂，反而是臺灣各地的觀光夜市。逛夜市在臺灣形成了特殊文化，也是很多人喜歡做的活動。全臺灣總共有 319 個鄉鎮，從北到南每一個鄉鎮都有大大小小的夜市，每一個夜市都反映在地特色。

They serve a variety of food and are the best place to explore Taiwanese snacks. You can eat glazed strawberries on the stick with a tiny red tomato at the end to clear away the sweetness, or you can try stinky tofu, Taiwanese omelet, or BBQ squid. The goods sold in night markets are economical and affordable. Many people like to "go around the night market" eating, buying clothing and toys, and playing fun games. It is the perfect place to pick up inexpensive souvenirs to take home. Go hungry and take cash!

夜市中會有各式各樣的臺灣小吃，更是探索臺灣小吃最佳地點，你可以吃一串草莓糖葫蘆，上面還有加一顆小小的紅番茄來清除口內的甜味，或者你可以試試臭豆腐、臺灣蚵仔煎、或烤魷魚。在夜市賣的商品都是經濟又實惠。很多人喜歡逛一趟夜市，吃的、穿的、玩的、用的全搞定。夜市是買便宜紀念品帶回家的理想地方。去夜市前要空著肚子，也不要忘了帶現金！

台灣夜市小吃

▶▶ 影子跟讀「短獨白填空」練習 🎧 MP3 001

除了前面的**「影子跟讀短獨白練習」**，現在試著在聽完對話後，完成下列填空練習，從中強化生活場景中常見的字彙以及拼字能力，答案的話請參照前面的獨白！

You can't visit Taiwan _____ _____ a night _____. Many tourists' _____ place is not the National Palace _____ or the CKS Memorial _____, but the night market. There are 319 _____ in Taiwan, each _____ their own _____ of the night market (large and small). Each night market _____ the _____ culture and food of the area.

你如果沒逛過夜市，就不能說你有來過臺灣，很多外國遊客最喜歡臺灣的地方不是故宮博物院或中正紀念堂，反而是臺灣各地的觀光夜市。逛夜市在臺灣形成了特殊文化，也是很多人喜歡做的活動。全臺灣總共有 319 個鄉鎮，從北到南每一個鄉鎮都有大大小小的夜市，每一個夜市都反映在地特色。

They _____ a _____ of food and are the best place to _____ Taiwanese _____. You can eat glazed _____ on the _____ with a tiny red _____ at the end to clear away the sweetness, or you can try _____ tofu, Taiwanese _____, or BBQ _____. The goods _____ in night markets are _____ and _____. Many people like to "go around the night market" eating, _____ clothing and toys, and playing fun _____. It is the _____ place to pick up _____ _____ to take home. Go _____ and take _____!

夜市中會有各式各樣的臺灣小吃，更是探索臺灣小吃最佳地點，你可以吃一串草莓糖葫蘆，上面還有加一顆小小的紅番茄來清除口內的甜味，或者你可以試試臭豆腐、臺灣蚵仔煎、或烤魷魚。在夜市賣的商品都是經濟又實惠。很多人喜歡逛一趟夜市，吃的、穿的、玩的、用的全搞定。夜市是買便宜紀念品帶回家的理想地方。去夜市前要空著肚子，也不要忘了帶現金！

UNIT ❷

特殊的「新竹風」

▶▶ 影子跟讀「短獨白」練習 🎧 MP3 002

此篇為「影子跟讀短獨白練習」，規劃了由聽「短獨白」的shadowing練習，強化聽力專注力和掌握各個考點，現在就一起動身，開始聽「短獨白」！

If you stay one day in Hsinchu, Taiwan, you will experience the power of the "screaming of the wind". Because Hsinchu is surrounded by mountains with one side facing the ocean, it has a special Hsinchu wind condition that is found nowhere else in Taiwan.

如果你有在臺灣新竹待過一整天，你就會體會到什麼是「風的尖叫聲」的力量。由於新竹主要是被山包圍但有一面是面向海，所以有特殊的「新竹風」，是在臺灣其他地方所沒有的。

The power of the wind is a natural condition that is critical when making rice vermicelli. The basic process is the following: make a rice dough, shred it, and cut it into noodles, then divide them and steam the noodles in a steamer where the rice vermicelli is partially cooked. But the final step requires the local wind. There is a lot of water involved during the process, so after the noodles are taken out of the steamer, it is placed in the sun where the powerful and special "Hsinchu wind" completely dries it.

　　「新竹風」的力量是製作米粉過程中最關鍵的自然條件。其基本製造過程包括做米糰、米粉壓絲、分割米粉，及在蒸籠蒸米粉，將米粉部分「煮熟」。最後一步則需要當地的風。在製造過程中有用很多的水，所以最後從蒸鍋中取出來之後，會將它放在太陽下，接受強大和特殊的「新竹風」來完全吹乾。

特殊的「新竹風」

▶ 影子跟讀「短獨白填空」練習 🎧 MP3 002

除了前面的**「影子跟讀短獨白練習」**，現在試著在聽完對話後，完成下列填空練習，從中強化生活場景中常見的字彙以及拼字能力，答案的話請參照前面的獨白！

If you stay one day _____ Hsinchu, Taiwan, you will _____ the _____ of the "screaming of the wind". Because Hsinchu is _____ by mountains _____ one side facing the _____, it has a _____ Hsinchu wind _____ that is found nowhere else in Taiwan.

　　如果你有在臺灣新竹待過一整天，你就會體會到什麼是「風的尖叫聲」的力量。由於新竹主要是被山包圍但有一面是面向海，所以有特殊的「新竹風」，是在臺灣其他地方所沒有的。

The _____ of the wind is a _____ _____ that is critical when making _____ vermicelli. The basic process is the following: make a rice _____, shred it, and cut it _____ _____, then _____ them and _____ the noodles in a _____ where the rice vermicelli is _____ cooked. But the _____ step requires the _____ wind. There is a lot of _____ involved _____ the _____, so after the noodles are taken out ____ the steamer, it is placed in the sun where the powerful and special "Hsinchu wind" _____ dries it.

「新竹風」的力量是製作米粉過程中最關鍵的自然條件。其基本製造過程包括做米糰、米粉壓絲、分割米粉,及在蒸籠蒸米粉,將米粉部分「煮熟」。最後一步則需要當地的風。在製造過程中有用很多的水,所以最後從蒸鍋中取出來之後,會將它放在太陽下,接受強大和特殊的「新竹風」來完全吹乾。

1
短獨白「影子跟讀」和填空練習

2
短獨白獨立演練和詳解

3
短獨白模擬試題

UNIT ❸

金門貢糖和高粱酒

此篇為**「影子跟讀短獨白練習」**，規劃了由聽**「短獨白」**的shad-owing練習，強化聽力專注力和掌握各個考點，現在就一起動身，開始聽**「短獨白」**！

Kinmen is a popular tourist destination that is known for quaint architecture and beaches. There are two specialty items a tourist should look for. The first is Kimen Peanut Candy. Many stores sell the peanut candy and most will encourage the buyer to try it before buying. However, buying the candy from a store that weighs it will give you more candy for the same price as the pre-boxed kind.

　　金門是一個有名的觀光景點，以古色古香的建築及其美麗的海灘而著稱。這裡有兩個旅客必看的項目。第一是金門貢糖。在金門街上有很多賣貢糖的店，很多店家也都會有試吃再買的服務，秤斤的貢糖會比較划算，秤斤與盒裝數量會差到至少二倍。

The second item is Kinmen Kaoliang Liquor which has a rich fragrance and is strong tasting. When compared to popular Taiwan alcohol, such as rice wine, wine, beer, and Shaoxing wine, the Kinmen Kaoliang Liquor has a higher alcohol concentration. Liquor in White Urn (with a 58.38 % alcoholic concentration) can only be bought in Kinmen. Warning: there are still mines in Kinmen. Although the mined area has signs, tourists still need to be careful and not mistakenly step on one!

再來是金門的高粱酒，因為氣候的關係以高粱釀出的酒醞育出芬芳氣味和濃郁口味，對於酒外行的遊客來説，到金門買高粱酒要注意的是，比起一般在臺灣普遍的米酒，葡萄酒，啤酒和紹興酒來説，酒精濃度高很多，像是只能在金門買到的白色甕裝，含有濃度 58%的酒精。金門的太陽很強烈，出門一定要注意防曬，另外要注意的就是金門現在還是有很多的地雷，雖然地雷區都會有標示，但是還是小心不要誤踩！

金門貢糖和高粱酒

▶▶ 影子跟讀「短獨白填空」練習 🎧 MP3 003

除了前面的**「影子跟讀短獨白練習」**，現在試著在聽完對話後，完成下列填空練習，從中強化生活場景中常見的字彙以及拼字能力，答案的話請參照前面的獨白！

Kinmen is a _____ tourist _____ that is known ____ _____ _____ and _____. There are two _____ items a tourist should look for. The first is Kimen Peanut Candy. Many _____ sell the peanut _____ and most will _____ the buyer to try it before buying. However, buying the candy _____ a store that _____ it will give you more candy _____ the same _____ as the _____ kind.

金門是一個有名的觀光景點，以古色古香的建築及其美麗的海灘而著稱。這裡有兩個旅客必看的項目。第一是金門貢糖。在金門街上有很多賣貢糖的店，很多店家也都會有試吃再買的服務，秤斤的貢糖會比較划算，秤斤與盒裝數量會差到至少二倍。

The second _____ is Kinmen Kaoliang Liquor which has a rich _____ and is _____ tasting. When _____ to popular Taiwan _____, such as rice wine, wine, beer, and Shaoxing wine, the Kinmen Kaoliang Liquor has a higher _____ _____. _____ in White Urn (____ a 58.38 % _____ concentration) can only be bought in Kinmen. Warning: there are still mines in Kinmen. Although the _____ area has signs, _____ still need ____ be careful and not _____ step on one!

再來是金門的高粱酒，因為氣候的關係以高粱釀出的酒醞育出芬芳氣味和濃郁口味，對於酒外行的遊客來說，到金門買高粱酒要注意的是，比起一般在臺灣普遍的米酒，葡萄酒，啤酒和紹興酒來說，酒精濃度高很多，像是只能在金門買到的白色甕裝，含有濃度 58%的酒精。金門的太陽很強烈，出門一定要注意防曬，另外要注意的就是金門現在還是有很多的地雷，雖然地雷區都會有標示，但是還是小心不要誤踩！

UNIT ④

臺灣烏龍茶

▶▶ 影子跟讀「短獨白」練習 🎧 MP3 004

　　此篇為「**影子跟讀短獨白練習**」，規劃了由聽「**短獨白**」的shadowing練習，強化聽力專注力和掌握各個考點，現在就一起動身，開始聽「**短獨白**」！

　　There are many different types of Taiwan oolong tea, such as Jin Xuan tea and Evergreen tea. Any tea that is fermented between 30 to 40 degrees Celsius can use the oolong tea label. Oolong's unique process is that after it's dried, the leaves are wrapped in a ball with a cloth and rolled back and forth until eventually the leaves are semi-fermented and hemispherical. Handpicked oolong tea leaves have one heart with three or two leaves. The final product is a hemispherical tea. After brewing, the tea is golden amber color and has a sweet taste.

　　臺灣烏龍茶的種類很多，例如金萱、松柏長青茶等，所有發酵三十至四十度之間做法的茶都可以被稱為烏龍茶。烏龍茶獨特的製茶過程是烘乾後再重複用布包成球狀揉捻茶葉，使茶葉呈半

發酵、半球狀。手工摘取的烏龍茶有一心三葉或一心兩葉，成品的茶葉是半球狀，沖泡後，茶是金黃偏琥珀色，回甘十足。

One type of Taiwanese oolong tea is Dongding Oolong Tea which is also known as Dongding Tea. Dongding Mountain is located near Unicorn Lake in Lugu Township, Nantou County, Taiwan. Dongding Oolong Tea is famous in Taiwan, but most people don't know it's named for Dongding Mountain.

凍頂烏龍茶就是一種臺灣烏龍茶，又稱凍頂茶，「凍頂」是地名，就是位在臺灣南投縣鹿谷鄉「麒麟潭」邊的「凍頂山」，凍頂烏龍茶在臺灣很有名但是很多人都不知道這個茶名就是來自真名的「凍頂山」。

UNIT ❹

臺灣烏龍茶

▶▶ 影子跟讀「短獨白填空」練習 🎧 MP3 004

　　除了前面的「**影子跟讀短獨白練習**」，現在試著在聽完對話後，完成下列填空練習，從中強化生活場景中常見的字彙以及拼字能力，答案的話請參照前面的獨白！

There are many _____ types of Taiwan oolong tea, such as Jin Xuan tea and Evergreen tea. Any tea that is _____ between 30 to 40 degrees _____ can use the oolong tea label. Oolong's unique process is that after it's dried, the _____ are _____ in a ball ____ a _____ and rolled back and forth until eventually the _____ are semi-fermented and _____. Handpicked oolong tea leaves have one _____ with three or two leaves. The final _____ is a hemispherical tea. After brewing, the tea is _____ _____ color and has a _____ taste.

　　臺灣烏龍茶的種類很多，例如金萱、松柏長青茶等，所有發酵三十至四十度之間做法的茶都可以被稱為烏龍茶。烏龍茶獨特的製茶過程是烘乾後再重複用布包成球狀揉捻茶葉，使茶葉呈半

發酵、半球狀。手工摘取的烏龍茶有一心三葉或一心兩葉，成品的茶葉是半球狀，沖泡後，茶是金黃偏琥珀色，回甘十足。

One _____ of Taiwanese oolong tea is Dongding Oolong Tea which is also known _____ Dongding Tea. Dongding Mountain is _____ near Unicorn Lake in Lugu Township, Nantou County, Taiwan. Dongding Oolong Tea is _____ in Taiwan, but most people don't know it's named _____ Dongding Mountain.

凍頂烏龍茶就是一種臺灣烏龍茶，又稱凍頂茶，「凍頂」是地名，就是位在臺灣南投縣鹿谷鄉「麒麟潭」邊的「凍頂山」，凍頂烏龍茶在臺灣很有名但是很多人都不知道這個茶名就是來自真名的「凍頂山」。

買茶葉小技巧

此篇為**「影子跟讀短獨白練習」**，規劃了由聽**「短獨白」**的shadowing練習，強化聽力專注力和掌握各個考點，現在就一起動身，開始聽**「短獨白」**！

Many tourist places in Taiwan sell tea and before purchasing, a tourist needs few key principles. In general, bigger tea leaves are hand-picked, while smaller tea leaves are machine harvested. The machine harvested tea is cheaper, while handpicked leaves are more expensive. If the tea feels dry and tingling, it means the leaves are well dried during the drying process. If the tea feels soft, it is possible that it wasn't dried enough.

在臺灣大部分的觀光地點都能買到茶葉，在購買茶葉之前需要掌握幾個原則。一般而言，顆粒較大的茶葉是手工採摘，顆粒細小的茶葉則可能是機器採收， 機器的茶菁品質不如手工採摘茶菁的注重與要求，所以價格也就略低。茶葉在製作完成時有一定的乾燥程度，如果用手摸茶時，感覺是乾燥且有刺刺的感覺，表

示乾燥程度良好，如果手摸到茶的感覺是軟軟的，可能乾燥不足或是受潮。

All tea should smell fresh without a bad smell or artificial flavors. With a good quality tea, even after the tea is cold, the aroma of the tea lingers. For a poorer quality tea, there is no aroma of the tea after it is cold. If you want to buy an expensive tea, ask the store to brew a cup for you to try before buying it.

任何的茶葉聞起來應該都有新鮮茶香，不應該有雜味或人工味道。不同的茶葉會有不同的茶湯色，基本上如果有渾濁不透明的茶湯色代表是不良品。茶沖泡熱水後都會有特有的茶香，如果有任何的異味都是不良品。上等的茶葉在泡完後放涼也會有香氣，劣等的茶葉在泡茶時會有香氣但是放涼後則消失。如果要購買高價的茶葉，可以要求店家當場試泡。

UNIT ❺

買茶葉小技巧

　　除了前面的「**影子跟讀短獨白練習**」，現在試著在聽完對話後，完成下列填空練習，從中強化生活場景中常見的字彙以及拼字能力，答案的話請參照前面的獨白！

　　Many tourist _____ in Taiwan sell tea and before _____, a tourist needs few key _____. In general, bigger tea leaves are _____, while _____ tea leaves are _____ harvested. The machine harvested tea is cheaper, while _____ leaves are more _____. If the tea feels dry and tingling, it means the leaves are well _____ during the _____ _____. If the tea feels soft, it is _____ that it wasn't dried enough.

　　在臺灣大部分的觀光地點都能買到茶葉，在購買茶葉之前需要掌握幾個原則。一般而言，顆粒較大的茶葉是手工採摘，顆粒細小的茶葉則可能是機器採收，機器的茶菁品質不如手工採摘茶菁的注重與要求，所以價格也就略低。茶葉在製作完成時有一定的乾燥程度，如果用手摸茶時，感覺是乾燥且有刺刺的感覺，表

示乾燥程度良好，如果手摸到茶的感覺是軟軟的，可能乾燥不足或是受潮。

All tea should smell _____ without a bad smell or _____ _____. With a good _____ tea, even after the tea is cold, the _____ of the tea _____. For a _____ _____ tea, there is no _____ of the tea after it is _____. If you want to buy an _____ tea, ask the store to brew a _____ for you to try before buying it.

　　任何的茶葉聞起來應該都有新鮮茶香，不應該有雜味或人工味道。不同的茶葉會有不同的茶湯色，基本上如果有渾濁不透明的茶湯色代表是不良品。茶沖泡熱水後都會有特有的茶香，如果有任何的異味都是不良品。上等的茶葉在泡完後放涼也會有香氣，劣等的茶葉在泡茶時會有香氣但是放涼後則消失。如果要購買高價的茶葉，可以要求店家當場試泡。

UNIT ❻

高山茶

▶️ **影子跟讀「短獨白」練習** 🎧 **MP3 006**

此篇為**「影子跟讀短獨白練習」**，規劃了由聽**「短獨白」**的shadowing練習，強化聽力專注力和掌握各個考點，現在就一起動身，開始聽**「短獨白」**！

High Mountain Tea" does not refer to a specific place. Basically, all tea grown at an altitude of 100 meters above sea level can be called "High Mountain Tea". Many of Taiwan's existing mountain tea farms originally grew trees or bamboo. Over the years, these lands accumulated organic materials which provide good nutrients for tea plants.

「高山茶」其實是一般名詞，並不是指特定地方所製作的茶葉。基本上，生長於海拔 1,000 公尺以上茶園所製的茶葉就是高山茶。臺灣現有的高山茶園很多以前是林地竹地，土壤裡充足的養份來自常年累積的有機質堆積，成為種茶的好地方。

There are two advantages to growing tea in the

high altitude. One is the cold climate and the short periods of daily sunshine, lowering the bitter components of tea and increasing the sweet taste. Second, due to the temperature difference between day and night and the long afternoon clouds, tea grows slowly which results in softer shoots and thicker mesophyll.

高山種茶還需要有兩項優勢，一是高山氣候的冷涼和平均較短的日照，這樣可以讓茶樹芽葉的苦澀成分降低而提升甘味。二是日夜溫差大及午後雲霧遮蔽會讓茶樹的生長趨於緩慢，讓芽葉柔軟和葉肉厚實。

高山茶

▶ 影子跟讀「短獨白填空」練習 🎧 MP3 006

除了前面的**「影子跟讀短獨白練習」**，現在試著在聽完對話後，完成下列填空練習，從中強化生活場景中常見的字彙以及拼字能力，答案的話請參照前面的獨白！

High Mountain Tea" does not refer _____ a _____ place. Basically, all tea _____ at an _____ of 100 meters above sea _____ can be called "High Mountain Tea". Many of Taiwan's _____ mountain tea farms _____ grew trees or bamboo. Over the years, these lands _____ _____ materials which _____ good _____ for tea _____.

「高山茶」其實是一般名詞，並不是指特定地方所製作的茶葉。基本上，生長於海拔 1,000 公尺以上茶園所製的茶葉就是高山茶。臺灣現有的高山茶園很多以前是林地竹地，土壤裡充足的養份來自常年累積的有機質堆積，成為種茶的好地方。

There are two _____ to growing tea _____ the high _____. One is the cold _____ and the short _____ of daily _____, lowering the _____ _____ of tea and increasing the _____ taste. Second, due _____ the _____ _____ between day and night and the long afternoon _____, tea grows _____ which results in _____ _____ and thicker mesophyll.

　　高山種茶還需要有兩項優勢，一是高山氣候的冷涼和平均較短的日照，這樣可以讓茶樹芽葉的苦澀成分降低而提升甘味。二是日夜溫差大及午後雲霧遮蔽會讓茶樹的生長趨於緩慢，讓芽葉柔軟和葉肉厚實。

UNIT ❼

貓空喫茶趣

▶ **影子跟讀「短獨白」練習** 🎧 **MP3 007**

此篇為**「影子跟讀短獨白練習」**，規劃了由聽**「短獨白」**的shadowing練習，強化聽力專注力和掌握各個考點，現在就一起動身，開始聽**「短獨白」**！

What's the first image that comes to your mind when you hear the word "Taipei"? I guess it might be the supertall skyscraper landmark- the Taipei 101, or maybe the antique architecture which displays so many ancient Chinese priceless treasures- the National Palace Museum. No matter what, I bet that you'll never associate agricultural production with Taipei. But in Maokong, the so-called "Taipei back garden", it is indeed renowned for its Paochong Tea.

當你聽到「臺北」的時候，第一個出現在腦海裡的景象是什麼呢？我猜想有可能是超高摩天大樓地標象徵的臺北 101，也或許是古色古香的建築中展示著許多中國古老稀世珍寶的故宮博物院吧。無論如何，我敢說你一定不會將臺北聯想到農產品上。一般被稱為是臺北後花園的貓空，真的是以其出產的包種茶而聞名。

The Taipei Promotion Center for Tie Kuanyin and Paochong Tea in Maokong is the perfect place for visitors to find out the full background on the development of the tea plantation in Muzha, Taipei. They offer the free-of-charge weekday education programs and weekend guided tours by volunteers. But, do not forget to make a reservation before your visit.

在貓空有一個臺北市鐵觀音包種茶推廣研發中心,在這裡,遊客可看到臺北木柵地區種茶發展的完整背景。他們有提供平日的教學觀摩課程及週末時的導覽,是由義工解說及免費的性質。但是不要忘記,在造訪茶中心之前一定要先預約。

貓空喫茶趣

▶▶ 影子跟讀「短獨白填空」練習 🎧 MP3 007

　　除了前面的「**影子跟讀短獨白練習**」，現在試著在聽完對話後，完成下列填空練習，從中強化生活場景中常見的字彙以及拼字能力，答案的話請參照前面的獨白！

　　What's the first _____ that comes _____ your _____ when you hear the word "Taipei"? I guess it might be the _____ _____ _____- the Taipei 101, or maybe the _____ _____ which _____ so many ancient Chinese _____ _____- the National Palace _____. No matter what, I bet that you'll never _____ _____ _____ with Taipei. But in Maokong, the so-called "Taipei back garden", it is indeed _____ for its Pao-chong Tea.

　　當你聽到「臺北」的時候，第一個出現在腦海裡的景象是什麼呢？我猜想有可能是超高摩天大樓地標象徵的臺北 101，也或許是古色古香的建築中展示著許多中國古老稀世珍寶的故宮博物院吧。無論如何，我敢說你一定不會將臺北聯想到農產品上。一

般被稱為是臺北後花園的貓空，真的是以其出產的包種茶而聞名。

The Taipei Promotion Center for Tie Kuanyin and Paochong Tea in Maokong is the _____ place for _____ to find out the full _____ on the _____ of the tea _____ in Muzha, Taipei. They offer the free-of-charge weekday _____ _____ and weekend _____ tours by _____. But, do not _____ to make a _____ before your visit.

　　在貓空有一個臺北市鐵觀音包種茶推廣研發中心，在這裡，遊客可看到臺北木柵地區種茶發展的完整背景。他們有提供平日的教學觀摩課程及週末時的導覽，是由義工解說及免費的性質。但是不要忘記，在造訪茶中心之前一定要先預約。

平價咖啡

▶▶ 影子跟讀「短獨白」練習 🎧 MP3 008

此篇為「**影子跟讀短獨白練習**」，規劃了由聽「**短獨白**」的shadowing練習，強化聽力專注力和掌握各個考點，現在就一起動身，開始聽「**短獨白**」！

If you want a cup of freshly-made coffee in the middle of the night in Taiwan, where do you go? 7-11, of course. 7-11 is everywhere in Taiwan and is open 24/7 all year around. The first 7-11 opened in 1980 in Taiwan, and since then, it has grown to more than 4,500 stores. Taiwan is only as large as the U.S. states of Maryland and Delaware combined, but in spite of the island's small size, 7-11 is big business. 7-11's inexpensive, convenient, and freshly-made coffee is very popular.

如果你在臺灣半夜三點有一股衝動想要喝一杯咖啡，你要去哪裡買？正確答案會是 7-11 便利店。7-11 在臺灣到處都有，也是 24/7 整年營業。1980 年時， 7-11 在臺灣開設了第一家，從那時起到到現在，已經開超過 4,500 家以上的7-11。臺灣的大

小大約只有美國馬里蘭州和德拉瓦州加起來。所以，儘管臺灣只是一個小小的島嶼，而 7-11 卻是一個相當大的企業。7-11 在 2004 年開始有CityCafé 咖啡廳，他們的平價，快速和現煮的咖啡已經變得非常流行。

When you order a cold latte at 7-11, the sales clerk puts packaged ice and milk in a cup under the coffee machine. When it's turned on, the beans are freshly ground, and the coffee is made within minutes of you ordering it. Plus, while you wait, you can mail a package, pay your bills, send a fax, and buy a snack.

在 7-11，當你點了冰拿鐵咖啡，店員會打開包裝好的冰塊和牛奶放在一個杯子放在咖啡機下，按下咖啡機後，就在你的眼前，咖啡機會把咖啡豆磨好，咖啡也會馬上泡好。然後，你可以在一兩分鐘內喝到很新鮮的咖啡。另外，當你在等咖啡時，你可以同時在店內寄包裹、付帳單、傳傳真，也可以買零食。

平價咖啡

▶▶ 影子跟讀「短獨白填空」練習 🎧 MP3 008

除了前面的**「影子跟讀短獨白練習」**，現在試著在聽完對話後，完成下列填空練習，從中強化生活場景中常見的字彙以及拼字能力，答案的話請參照前面的獨白！

If you want a cup of _____ coffee in the _____ of the night in Taiwan, where do you go? 7-11, of course. 7-11 is everywhere in Taiwan and is open 24/7 all year around. The first 7-11 opened in _____ in Taiwan, and since then, it has _____ to more than 4,500 _____. Taiwan is only as _____ as the U.S. states of _____ and Delaware combined, but in spite of the _____ small size, 7-11 is big business. 7-11's _____, convenient, and _____ coffee is very _____.

如果你在臺灣半夜三點有一股衝動想要喝一杯咖啡，你要去哪裡買？正確答案會是 7-11 便利店。7-11 在臺灣到處都有，也是 24/7 整年營業。1980 年時，7-11 在臺灣開設了第一家，從那時起到到現在，已經開超過 4,500 家以上的7-11。臺灣的大

小大約只有美國馬里蘭州和德拉瓦州加起來。所以，儘管臺灣只是一個小小的島嶼，而 7-11 卻是一個相當大的企業。7-11 在 2004 年開始有CityCafé 咖啡廳，他們的平價，快速和現煮的咖啡已經變得非常流行。

When you order a cold _____ at 7-11, the sales _____ puts _____ ice and _____ in a cup under the coffee _____. When it's turned on, the _____ are freshly ground, and the coffee is made within _____ of you ordering it. Plus, while you wait, you can mail a _____, pay your bills, send a _____, and buy a _____.

在 7-11，當你點了冰拿鐵咖啡，店員會打開包裝好的冰塊和牛奶放在一個杯子放在咖啡機下，按下咖啡機後，就在你的眼前，咖啡機會把咖啡豆磨好，咖啡也會馬上泡好。然後，你可以在一兩分鐘內喝到很新鮮的咖啡。另外，當你在等咖啡時，你可以同時在店內寄包裹、付帳單、傳傳真，也可以買零食。

買咖啡體驗

▶ 影子跟讀「短獨白」練習 🎧 MP3 009

此篇為「影子跟讀短獨白練習」，規劃了由聽「短獨白」的shadowing練習，強化聽力專注力和掌握各個考點，現在就一起動身，開始聽「短獨白」！

In Taiwan, you can buy inexpensive coffee everywhere - at convenience stores and at the major coffee chain stores. These highly advertised shops not only serve cheap coffee, but most grind the coffee fresh and are concerned about the quality of the coffee. Their goal is to serve inexpensive high quality coffee quickly. Some of the bigger coffee shops have coffee roasting machines, while other stores sell a wide variety of coffee making equipment to use at home.

在臺灣到處都可以買到平價咖啡，便利商店和大型咖啡連鎖店都可以買到平價咖啡。這些有名的店不僅賣便宜的咖啡，很多是現磨現煮，也都非常注重品質。他們的目標就是要賣快速高品質的平價咖啡。有大型的店還會擺設咖啡烘焙機，也會賣一些可以家庭用的泡咖啡器具。

However, the best thing to do is to go exploring and find the small coffee shops in the alleys and lanes of the big cities. This type of coffee shop is usually quite small, and the decor of the coffee shop reflects the owner's taste. Coffee enthusiasts share their experiences with the small coffee shops in blogs and in reviews online, making it easy for tourists to find the perfect cup of coffee.

其實如果你有閒情逸致的話，很多大城市裡不起眼的小巷弄裡會有很多有特色的咖啡店，這類型的特色都是小小的，但通常會表現出老闆自己品味的特色。網路上很容易找到這樣的資料，很多個人部落格裡也會分享自己對這些巷弄裡的咖啡店的經驗。咖啡愛好者會在部落格分享他們在小咖啡店的經驗，也會在網路寫評論，這些資料可以讓遊客很方便的尋找一杯完美的咖啡。

買咖啡體驗

▶▶ **影子跟讀「短獨白填空」練習** 🎧 **MP3 009**

除了前面的**「影子跟讀短獨白練習」**，現在試著在聽完對話後，完成下列填空練習，從中強化生活場景中常見的字彙以及拼字能力，答案的話請參照前面的獨白！

In Taiwan, you can buy _____ coffee everywhere - at _____ stores and at the _____ coffee chain stores. These highly _____ shops not only serve cheap coffee, but most _____ the coffee fresh and are _____ about the _____ of the coffee. Their goal is to serve inexpensive high _____ coffee quickly. Some of the bigger coffee shops have coffee roasting machines, while other _____ sell a _____ variety of coffee making _____ to use at _____.

在臺灣到處都可以買到平價咖啡，便利商店和大型咖啡連鎖店都可以買到平價咖啡。這些有名的店不僅賣便宜的咖啡，很多是現磨現煮，也都非常注重品質。他們的目標就是要賣快速高品質的平價咖啡。有大型的店還會擺設咖啡烘焙機，也會賣一些可

以家庭用的泡咖啡器具。

However, the best thing to do is to go _____ and find the small coffee shops in the _____ and _____ of the big cities. This type of coffee shop is _____ quite small, and the _____ of the coffee shop _____ the owner's _____. Coffee _____ share their experiences with the small coffee shops in _____ and in _____ online, making it _____ for tourists to find the _____ cup of cof-fee.

其實如果你有閒情逸致的話,很多大城市裡不起眼的小巷弄裡會有很多有特色的咖啡店,這類型的特色都是小小的,但通常會表現出老闆自己品味的特色。網路上很容易找到這樣的資料,很多個人部落格裡也會分享自己對這些巷弄裡的咖啡店的經驗。咖啡愛好者會在部落格分享他們在小咖啡店的經驗,也會在網路寫評論,這些資料可以讓遊客很方便的尋找一杯完美的咖啡。

古坑咖啡

▶ 影子跟讀「短獨白」練習　🎧 MP3 010

此篇為「影子跟讀短獨白練習」，規劃了由聽「短獨白」的shad-owing練習，強化聽力專注力和掌握各個考點，現在就一起動身，開始聽「短獨白」！

Locally grown coffee in Taiwan? Really? Yes! The home of Taiwanese coffee is in the Huashan area of Gukeng County in Yunlin, Taiwan. The Dutch brought coffee to Taiwan in 1924, but Japanese started growing coffee in Taiwan in 1941. They found the best place to grow coffee was in Gukeng County. After the war and the Japanese left Taiwan, the price for coffee beans wasn't competitive enough, so many coffee plantations were abandoned.

臺灣本土咖啡？真的嗎？真的。臺灣咖啡原產地是在臺灣雲林古坑縣的華山地區。臺灣最早的咖啡是由荷蘭人於 1924 年所引進，日本人在臺灣在 1941 年開始種植咖啡，他們發在古坑縣是種植咖啡的最佳場所。戰後日本人離開臺灣後，咖啡的價格沒有競爭性所以後來該地區大多數的咖啡種植園都荒廢了。

But in 2000, the Taiwanese government encouraged local growers to cultivate locally grown coffee again. The first Coffee Festival in Taiwan was held in Yunlin, in 2003, and "Gukeng Coffee" (a type of Arabica coffee) started gaining its reputation. After that, Taiwanese Coffee developed a market share. Although a lot of coffee is still imported in Taiwan, the locally grown coffee has the distinct taste due to different roasting, extraction method, and brewing time. Try a cup of Gukeng Coffee during your visit!

直到 2000 年，臺灣政府開始鼓勵當地人種植臺灣本地咖啡。在 2003 年，臺灣第一季咖啡節是在雲林舉行，「古坑咖啡」（阿拉比卡咖啡的種類）開始獲得聲譽。之後，臺灣咖啡開始在市場上佔有一席之地。雖然在臺灣有很多進口咖啡，當地種植的咖啡因為有不同的烘焙和萃取的方法所以具有特殊的味道。如果有機會的話，別忘了來一杯古坑咖啡！

古坑咖啡

▶ 影子跟讀「短獨白填空」練習　🎧 MP3 010

　　除了前面的**「影子跟讀短獨白練習」**，現在試著在聽完對話後，完成下列填空練習，從中強化生活場景中常見的字彙以及拼字能力，答案的話請參照前面的獨白！

　　_____ grown coffee in Taiwan? Really? Yes! The _____ of Taiwanese coffee is in the Huashan area of Gukeng County in Yunlin, Taiwan. The Dutch brought coffee _____ Taiwan in _____, but _____ started growing coffee in Taiwan in 1941. They found the best place to grow coffee was in Gukeng County. After the _____ and the Japanese left Taiwan, the price _____ coffee _____ wasn't _____ enough, so many coffee _____ were _____.

　　臺灣本土咖啡？真的嗎？真的。臺灣咖啡原產地是在臺灣雲林古坑縣的華山地區。臺灣最早的咖啡是由荷蘭人於 1924 年所引進，日本人在臺灣在 1941 年開始種植咖啡，他們發在古坑縣是種植咖啡的最佳場所。戰後日本人離開臺灣後，咖啡的價格沒有競爭性所以後來該地區大多數的咖啡種植園都荒廢了。

But in 2000, the Taiwanese _____ _____ local growers to cultivate locally grown coffee again. The first Coffee _____ in Taiwan was held in Yunlin, in 2003, and "Gukeng Coffee" (a type of Arabica coffee) started _____ its _____. After that, Taiwanese Coffee _____ a market share. Although a lot of coffee is still _____ in Taiwan, the locally grown coffee has the _____ taste due to different _____, extraction _____, and _____ time. Try a cup of Gukeng Coffee during your visit!

直到 2000 年，臺灣政府開始鼓勵當地人種植臺灣本地咖啡。在 2003 年，臺灣第一季咖啡節是在雲林舉行，「古坑咖啡」（阿拉比卡咖啡的種類）開始獲得聲譽。之後，臺灣咖啡開始在市場上佔有一席之地。雖然在臺灣有很多進口咖啡，當地種植的咖啡因為有不同的烘焙和萃取的方法所以具有特殊的味道。如果有機會的話，別忘了來一杯古坑咖啡！

庵古坑和橙之鄉

▶ 影子跟讀「短獨白」練習　🎧 MP3 011

此篇為「影子跟讀短獨白練習」，規劃了由聽「短獨白」的shadowing練習，強化聽力專注力和掌握各個考點，現在就一起動身，開始聽「短獨白」！

In the past, Gukeng County was called Um Gukeng. Because of its climate and geology, Gukeng County is the main agricultural area in Taiwan. In recent years, this county became famous for its locally grown coffee, but many other agricultural crops grow here as well. The oranges grown here are the best in Taiwan and have given the county the nickname of Orange County. Beside oranges, other fruits grown here, such as grapefruit, mandarin oranges, and pineapple, are also outstanding. A lot of the fruit orchards encourage tourists to come and pick their own fruit right off the trees.

古坑鄉以前叫做「庵古坑」(Um Gukeng)，因為氣候和地質的關係，這裡是臺灣農業主要的產區，近年除了出產臺灣咖啡而大有名氣外，許多其他的農作物也耕種於此，這裡的柳丁產量也

是全臺之冠,良好的柳丁品質讓這裡有了「橙之鄉」的美譽。除了柳丁之外,還有葡萄柚、柑桔、鳳梨都是很出色的當地出產水果,這裡有很多的觀光果園可以讓遊客享受採收的樂趣。

Flowers from the citrus plants bloom from March to April in Um Gukeng, and a sea of white flowers from the citrus trees cover the whole town of Um Gukeng. When you are planning a trip to Um Gukeng, don't forget to include the annual blossom season.

「庵古坑」每年到了 3～4 月時就是柑橘類花朵盛開的時候,果樹上的花望眼看去好像鋪蓋了整個古坑,在做行程的設計時不要忘了考慮一年才開一次的橙花季節。

1 短獨白「影子跟讀」和填空練習

2 短獨白獨立演練和詳解

3 短獨白模擬試題

UNIT ⑪

庵古坑和橙之鄉

　　除了前面的**「影子跟讀短獨白練習」**，現在試著在聽完對話後，完成下列填空練習，從中強化生活場景中常見的字彙以及拼字能力，答案的話請參照前面的獨白！

　　In the past, Gukeng County was called Um Gukeng. Because _____ its _____ and _____, Gukeng County is the main _____ area in Taiwan. In recent years, this county became _____ for its locally grown coffee, but many other _____ _____ grow here as well. The _____ grown here are the best in Taiwan and have _____ the county the _____ of Orange County. Beside oranges, other fruits grown here, such as _____, _____ oranges, and _____, are also _____. A lot of the fruit _____ encourage tourists to come and pick their own fruit right off the trees.

　　古坑鄉以前叫做「庵古坑」(Um Gukeng)，因為氣候和地質的關係，這裡是臺灣農業主要的產區，近年除了出產臺灣咖啡而

大有名氣外，許多其他的農作物也耕種於此，這裡的柳丁產量也是全臺之冠，良好的柳丁品質讓這裡有了「橙之鄉」的美譽。除了柳丁之外，還有葡萄柚、柑桔、鳳梨都是很出色的當地出產水果，這裡有很多的觀光果園可以讓遊客享受採收的樂趣。

Flowers from the citrus plants _____ from _____ to _____ in Um Gukeng, and a sea of _____ flowers from the _____ trees cover the _____ town of Um Gukeng. When you are _____ a trip to Um Gukeng, don't forget to _____ the _____ _____ season.

「庵古坑」每年到了 3～4 月時就是柑橘類花朵盛開的時候，果樹上的花望眼看去好像鋪蓋了整個古坑，在做行程的設計時不要忘了考慮一年才開一次的橙花季節。

惠蓀咖啡

▶▶ **影子跟讀「短獨白」練習** 🎧 MP3 012

此篇為**「影子跟讀短獨白練習」**，規劃了由聽**「短獨白」**的shad-owing練習，強化聽力專注力和掌握各個考點，現在就一起動身，開始聽**「短獨白」**！

The Arabica coffee bean grown at the Huisun Farm was first introduced by Japanese in 1936. The Huisin Farm has rich natural resources perfect for growing coffee but natural conditions, such as earthquakes, typhoons, and insect infestations destroy coffee plants and beans and affect the crops. A teaching and research farm, its main purpose is to promote local grown coffee as well as to assist farmers. Because the coffee from Huisun Farm is 100% locally grown, it tastes different from imported coffee due to the different climates and soils it's grown in. The end result is a neutral sweet taste full of aroma.

惠蓀林場的阿拉比卡咖啡豆最早是由日本人在 1936 引進種植。蕙蓀林場的所在地的自然資源相當豐富，但是卻要克服種種

的天然條件，如地震，風災，還有害蟲入侵會破壞咖啡樹和咖啡豆，進而影響農作物的生長。這是一個以學校生態植物教學研究為主，主要目的是提倡本土咖啡的種植和教育農夫，因為惠蓀林場的咖啡百分之百產自於臺灣本土，也因氣候、水土等各方面不同，口味與進口之咖啡豆相比顯得中性、甘味、香氣十足。

In 2003, the official name for the coffee from Huisun is called "Taiwan Huisun Coffee" which is abbreviated HS. This is a developing industry, and as farmers plant more coffee trees, set up more processing plants, refine the bean quality, and develop a market for the locally grown coffee, it will expand.

在 2003 年正式以「臺灣惠蓀咖啡」行銷，惠蓀咖啡的縮寫是「HS」。這是一個發展中的行業，當農民種植更多的咖啡樹、設立了加工廠、精鍊咖啡豆的品質，並開發出當地種植咖啡的市場時，臺灣咖啡也將擴大佔領市場。

UNIT ⑫

惠蓀咖啡

▶▶ 影子跟讀「短獨白填空」練習 🎧 MP3 012

除了前面的「**影子跟讀短獨白練習**」，現在試著在聽完對話後，完成下列填空練習，從中強化生活場景中常見的字彙以及拼字能力，答案的話請參照前面的獨白！

The Arabica coffee bean grown _____ the Huisun Farm was first _____ by Japanese in _____. The Huisin Farm has _____ _____ resources _____ for growing coffee but _____ conditions, such _____ _____, _____, and insect _____ _____ coffee plants and beans and affect the crops. A teaching and research farm, its main _____ is to _____ local grown coffee as well as to _____ farmers. Because the coffee from Huisun Farm is 100% locally grown, it tastes _____ from imported coffee due to the different _____ and soils it's grown in. The _____ result is a _____ sweet taste full of _____.

惠蓀林場的阿拉比卡咖啡豆最早是由日本人在 1936 引進種

植。蕙蓀林場的所在地的自然資源相當豐富，但是卻要克服種種的天然條件，如地震，風災，還有害蟲入侵會破壞咖啡樹和咖啡豆，進而影響農作物的生長。這是一個以學校生態植物教學研究為主，主要目的是提倡本土咖啡的種植和教育農夫，因為惠蓀林場的咖啡百分之百產自於臺灣本土，也因氣候、水土等各方面不同，口味與進口之咖啡豆相比顯得中性、甘味、香氣十足。

In 2003, the _____ name for the coffee from Huisun is called "Taiwan Huisun Coffee" which is _____ HS. This is a _____ industry, and as farmers plant more coffee trees, set up more _____ plants, _____ the bean quality, and develop a _____ for the locally grown coffee, it will _____.

在 2003 年正式以「臺灣惠蓀咖啡」行銷，惠蓀咖啡的縮寫是「HS」。這是一個發展中的行業，當農民種植更多的咖啡樹、設立了加工廠、精鍊咖啡豆的品質，並開發出當地種植咖啡的市場時，臺灣咖啡也將擴大佔領市場。

UNIT ⓭

北投溫泉

▶▶ 影子跟讀「短獨白」練習 🎧 MP3 013

此篇為「影子跟讀短獨白練習」，規劃了由聽「短獨白」的shadowing練習，強化聽力專注力和掌握各個考點，現在就一起動身，開始聽「短獨白」！

Imagine soaking at a naturally formed hot springs pool with the steam rising from valley below in cold weather. Sounds like Heaven! In 1896, the Japanese built the first hot springs hotel in Taiwan called "Tengu Um house" in Bei Tou. They wanted to provide a place for the Japanese soldiers similar to the hot springs bath they had at home. It is still in business after all these years, but the name has changed to "Takimoto". A small monument stands in the front yard to commemorate the visit from the Crown Prince of Japan in 1923.

　　想想看，如果可以在冬天時，浸泡在自然形成的溫泉，而其蒸汽則是從下面的山谷所冒出，這聽起來是不是很像身在天堂！1896 年日本人在北投溫泉設立了臺灣第一家溫泉旅社叫「天狗庵旅舍」，就是目前還繼續經營的「瀧乃湯」。當時建立的目的

主要是讓在臺灣的日本軍可以有泡湯的地方。在院子裡還可以看到「皇太子殿下御渡涉紀念碑」，這是紀念 1923 年日本皇太子裕仁來臺視察時有實際來到北投。

Since it was built by Japanese, the architecture is quite unique when compared with the other large spa hotels in the area. In "Takimoto", there are separated baths for men and women. The naturally formed hot springs bath is very attractive to the visitors historically. Plus the low fee makes you want to return like the local regular visitors do.

瀧乃湯因為歷史悠久所以其日式建築與當今很多的大型溫泉會館比較下是很獨特的。這裡有分男女浴池，瀧乃湯裡自然形成的浴池，其歷史性是很吸引人的，還有，這裡的價格非常的平價，這樣的平價會讓你和當地人一樣會想定期的去泡湯。

UNIT ⓵③

北投溫泉

▶ 影子跟讀「短獨白填空」練習 🎧 MP3 013

　　除了前面的**「影子跟讀短獨白練習」**，現在試著在聽完對話後，完成下列填空練習，從中強化生活場景中常見的字彙以及拼字能力，答案的話請參照前面的獨白！

　　Imagine _____ at a _____ formed hot springs _____ ____ the steam rising ____ _____ below in cold _____. Sounds like _____! In 1896, the Japanese built the first hot springs _____ in Taiwan called "Tengu Um house" in Bei Tou. They wanted to _____ a place ____ the Japanese _____ _____ to the hot springs _____ they had at home. It is still in business after all these years, but the name has changed to "Takimoto". A small _____ stands in the front yard to _____ the visit ____ the Crown _____ of Japan in 1923.

　　想想看，如果可以在冬天時，浸泡在自然形成的溫泉，而其蒸汽則是從下面的山谷所冒出，這聽起來是不是很像身在天堂！1896 年日本人在北投溫泉設立了臺灣第一家溫泉旅社叫「天狗

庵旅舍」，就是目前還繼續經營的「瀧乃湯」。當時建立的目的主要是讓在臺灣的日本軍可以有泡湯的地方。在院子裡還可以看到「皇太子殿下御渡涉紀念碑」，這是紀念 1923 年日本皇太子裕仁來臺視察時有實際來到北投。

Since it was built by Japanese, the _____ is quite _____ when compared ____ the other _____ spa hotels in the area. In "Takimoto", there are _____ baths ____ men and women. The naturally formed hot springs bath is very _____ to the visitors _____. Plus the low fee makes you want to _____ like the local _____ visitors do.

　　瀧乃湯因為歷史悠久所以其日式建築與當今很多的大型溫泉會館比較下是很獨特的。這裡有分男女浴池，瀧乃湯裡自然形成的浴池，其歷史性是很吸引人的，還有，這裡的價格非常的平價，這樣的平價會讓你和當地人一樣會想定期的去泡湯。

北投一日遊

▶ 影子跟讀「短獨白」練習 🎧 MP3 014

此篇為「影子跟讀短獨白練習」，規劃了由聽「短獨白」的shadowing練習，強化聽力專注力和掌握各個考點，現在就一起動身，開始聽「短獨白」！

Bei Tou Hot Springs area is worth a day tour with many famous tourist places. The New Bei Tou Hot Springs Museum is only about three minutes away from MRT. In the museum, you will see the hot springs culture and history. Not far away from the Hot Springs Museum, there is an open-air Japanese-style public hot springs pool. It is an inexpensive way to experience the traditional Japanese open-air hot spring pool. In the Hot Springs Water Park, there is a Japanese-style wooden bridge and gazebo. There is also a free hot spring "foot spa" area so that visitors can really get into water.

北投溫泉區內有不少古蹟名勝很值得做一日遊。北投溫泉博物館距離新北投捷運站約三分鐘的路程。在博物館裡可以看到北

投溫泉悠久的文化與歷史。就在溫泉博物館上方不遠處，有一個露天日式公共溫泉池，這個公共浴池的收費非常低，是一個可以體驗便宜又露天的泡湯地方。北投溫泉親水公園內可以看到日式風格的木製拱橋、涼亭，也有免費溫泉「泡腳區」，讓遊客能真的「親水」。

The Taipei Public Library Bei Tou Branch is Taiwan's first green library building. The building is designed to be environment friendly with solar power and a rain-water recycling system. Of course, you should try the local food for your day trip. Bei Tou's "Jiu Jia Cai" ("special restaurant food") is very unique. There were a lot of exclusive restaurants in the 1950s, and wealthy politicians and business people came here to drink and entertain guests and business associates. The menu slowly developed into luxurious gourmet Chinese dishes.

臺北市立圖書館北投分館是臺灣第一座綠建築的圖書館，這個建築是以太陽能發電及雨水回收系統的環保概念所設計的。一日遊當然不能忘記美食，北投的「酒家菜」是很有特色的。1950年代的北投有很多的酒家，很多政商和富商名流都會來此飲酒作樂，慢慢的就形成了獨特風格的酒家菜。

UNIT ⑭

北投一日遊

▶▶ **影子跟讀「短獨白填空」練習** 🎧 MP3 014

　　除了前面的**「影子跟讀短獨白練習」**，現在試著在聽完對話後，完成下列填空練習，從中強化生活場景中常見的字彙以及拼字能力，答案的話請參照前面的獨白！

　　Bei Tou Hot Springs area is _____ a day tour with many _____ tourist places. The New Bei Tou Hot Springs Museum is only about three _____ away from MRT. In the museum, you will see the hot springs _____ and history. Not far away from the Hot Springs Museum, there is an open-air Japanese-style _____ hot springs pool. It is an _____ way to _____ the _____ Japanese open-air hot spring pool. In the Hot Springs Water Park, there is a Japanese-style _____ _____ and gazebo. There is also a free hot spring "foot spa" area _____ that _____ can really get into _____.

　　北投溫泉區內有不少古蹟名勝很值得做一日遊。北投溫泉博物館距離新北投捷運站約三分鐘的路程。在博物館裡可以看到北

投溫泉悠久的文化與歷史。就在溫泉博物館上方不遠處，有一個露天日式公共溫泉池，這個公共浴池的收費非常低，是一個可以體驗便宜又露天的泡湯地方。北投溫泉親水公園內可以看到日式風格的木製拱橋、涼亭，也有免費溫泉「泡腳區」，讓遊客能真的「親水」。

The Taipei Public Library Bei Tou Branch is Taiwan's first green library _____. The building is _____ to be _____ friendly ____ _____ power and a _____ _____ system. Of course, you should try the _____ food for your day trip. Bei Tou's "Jiu Jia Cai" ("special restaurant food") is very _____. There were a lot of _____ _____ in the 1950s, and _____ _____ and business people came here to drink and _____ guests and business _____. The menu _____ developed into _____ _____ Chinese dishes.

臺北市立圖書館北投分館是臺灣第一座綠建築的圖書館，這個建築是以太陽能發電及雨水回收系統的環保概念所設計的。一日遊當然不能忘記美食，北投的「酒家菜」是很有特色的。1950年代的北投有很多的酒家，很多政商和富商名流都會來此飲酒作樂，慢慢的就形成了獨特風格的酒家菜。

UNIT ⑮

知本溫泉

此篇為**「影子跟讀短獨白練習」**，規劃了由聽**「短獨白」**的shadowing練習，強化聽力專注力和掌握各個考點，現在就一起動身，開始聽**「短獨白」**！

Nestled in the Central Mountains, surrounded by metamorphic slate, in the middle of nature, is the Jhihben hot springs in Beinan Township in Taitung. Many think "Jhihben" was named by the Japanese, but "Jhihben" is originally from the aboriginal word "Kadibu" which sounded like "Jhihben", "Dibun" in the Taiwanese dialect.

知本溫泉位於臺灣臺東縣卑南鄉，知本溫泉屬於位於中央山脈板岩區的變質岩區溫泉。很多臺灣人以為「知本」是由日人所命名，但是「知本」其實是原住民語「卡地布」(Kadibu)，臺語中聽起來就有點像是「知本」(Dibun)。

Aboriginal people found the Jhihben hot springs a

long time ago, but during the Japanese occupation in Taiwan, they constructed some public bathhouses and hotels in the area. The Jhihben hot springs water temperature can get up to 95°C with pH value of about pH 8.5. The water contains bicarbonate ions around 627-1816 ppm and sodium ions of about 419-951 ppm and is a neutral sodium bicarbonate springs. Colorless and odorless, the mineral springs are a pleasant way to enjoy the beautiful mountain scenery.

當地的原住民在很早以前就發現了知本溫泉，日本人只是在日據時代在這裡建設公共澡堂與賓館。知本溫泉的水溫最高可達 95°C，酸鹼值約 pH 8.5，含碳酸氫根離子約 627-1816 ppm，鈉離子約 419-951 ppm，屬於中性碳酸氫鈉泉。無色無味，這樣的溫泉是享受美麗山林風景的絕妙方式。

UNIT ⑮

知本溫泉

▶▶ **影子跟讀「短獨白填空」練習** 🎧 **MP3 015**

除了前面的**「影子跟讀短獨白練習」**，現在試著在聽完對話後，完成下列填空練習，從中強化生活場景中常見的字彙以及拼字能力，答案的話請參照前面的獨白！

_____ in the Central Mountains, surrounded ____ _____ slate, in the middle of _____, is the Jhihben hot springs in Beinan _____ in Taitung. Many think "Jhihben" was _____ by the Japanese, but "Jhihben" is originally from the _____ word "Kadibu" which sounded like "Jhihben", "Dibun" in the Taiwanese _____.

知本溫泉位於臺灣臺東縣卑南鄉，知本溫泉屬於位於中央山脈板岩區的變質岩區溫泉。很多臺灣人以為「知本」是由日人所命名，但是「知本」其實是原住民語「卡地布」(Kadibu)，臺語中聽起來就有點像是「知本」(Dibun)。

Aboriginal people found the Jhihben hot springs a

_____ time ago, but _____ the Japanese _____ in Taiwan, they _____ some public _____ and hotels in the area. The Jhihben hot springs water _____ can get up to 95℃ _____ pH _____ of about pH 8.5. The water _____ bicarbonate ions around 627-1816 ppm and _____ ions of about 419-951 ppm and is a _____ sodium bicarbonate springs. _____ and _____, the _____ springs are a _____ way to enjoy the _____ mountain _____.

當地的原住民在很早以前就發現了知本溫泉，日本人只是在日據時代在這裡建設公共澡堂與賓館。知本溫泉的水溫最高可達 95℃，酸鹼值約 pH 8.5，含碳酸氫根離子約 627-1816 ppm，鈉離子約 419-951 ppm，屬於中性碳酸氫鈉泉。無色無味，這樣的溫泉是享受美麗山林風景的絕妙方式。

礁溪溫泉

▶▶ 影子跟讀「短獨白」練習　🎧 MP3 016

　　此篇為「影子跟讀短獨白練習」，規劃了由聽「短獨白」的shadowing練習，強化聽力專注力和掌握各個考點，現在就一起動身，開始聽「短獨白」！

　　Get back to nature by visiting one of the best hot springs, Jaiosi, in Ilan. Because of special geological formations, it is a rare ground level hot springs. The rising steam from the underground heat joins with the ground water leaving a water so pure that it has multiple uses. The hot springs water is clear and odorless and has a neutral quality pH value between 7.2–7.9.

　　宜蘭礁溪最好的溫泉可以讓你感覺環繞在自然的懷抱裡。宜蘭礁溪因為特殊的地質構造，成為少見的平地溫泉。因為地下有熱源，上升的熱氣結合地下水之後產生多用途的泉水，這裡的溫泉青色無味，水質呈中性，pH 值在 7.2–7.9 之間。

　　The average water temperature is 50 degrees Celsius. The hot springs not only are used for spa and regular bath, after water treatment, the hot spring water here is also drinkable. Because it is ground level hot springs, visitors don't have to go all the way up to the mountains to enjoy the valley hot springs. The smart people of Ilan also use this type of neutral water to grow vegetables, make water drinkable, and to develop a unique aquaculture industry.

平均水溫約在攝氏 50 度。礁溪的泉水不僅可以供作泡溫泉，洗澡的用途，在經過處理後也可以當礦泉水飲用，也因為是平地溫泉，更是讓人覺得不需翻山越嶺就可以享受到溫泉。而聰明的宜蘭人也利用這樣的中性的水質發展出很特別的溫泉蔬菜、可供飲用的溫泉水、以及溫泉養殖的產業。

礁溪溫泉

▶▶ 影子跟讀「短獨白填空」練習 🎧 MP3 016

　　除了前面的**「影子跟讀短獨白練習」**，現在試著在聽完對話後，完成下列填空練習，從中強化生活場景中常見的字彙以及拼字能力，答案的話請參照前面的獨白！

　　Get back to nature by visiting one _____ the best hot springs, Jaiosi, in Ilan. Because of _____ _____ _____, it is a _____ ground level hot springs. The rising _____ from the _____ heat _____ with the ground water leaving a water so pure that it has multiple uses. The hot springs water is clear and _____ and has a _____ quality pH value between 7.2–7.9.

　　宜蘭礁溪最好的溫泉可以讓你感覺環繞在自然的懷抱裡。宜蘭礁溪因為特殊的地質構造，成為少見的平地溫泉。因為地下有熱源，上升的熱氣結合地下水之後產生多用途的泉水，這裡的溫泉青色無味，水質呈中性，pH 值在 7.2–7.9 之間。

The _____ water temperature is 50 degrees _____. The hot springs not only are _____ for spa and _____ bath, after water _____, the hot spring water here is also _____. Because it is _____ level hot springs, _____ don't have to go all the way up ____ the mountains to enjoy the _____ hot springs. The smart people of Ilan also use this type of _____ water to grow _____, make water _____, and to _____ a unique _____ industry.

平均水溫約在攝氏 50 度。礁溪的泉水不僅可以供作泡溫泉，洗澡的用途，在經過處理後也可以當礦泉水飲用，也因為是平地溫泉，更是讓人覺得不需翻山越嶺就可以享受到溫泉。而聰明的宜蘭人也利用這樣的中性的水質發展出很特別的溫泉蔬菜、可供飲用的溫泉水、以及溫泉養殖的產業。

礁溪溫泉公園

▶▶ 影子跟讀「短獨白」練習　🎧 MP3 017

　　此篇為「影子跟讀短獨白練習」，規劃了由聽「短獨白」的shadowing練習，強化聽力專注力和掌握各個考點，現在就一起動身，開始聽「短獨白」！

　　There are many hot spring water gushes near the downtown train station in Ilan. If you walk around town, you will see several free foot spas. There are three hot springs parks in Jaohsi that offer a free foot spa. Tangweigou Park is near the train station in Jiaosi, right by the main road. It is a unique park that is designed to make visitors take off their shoes and soak in the water of the foot spas.

　　在宜蘭市區的火車站口附近就有很多溫泉自然湧出，礁溪鎮上繞一圈就可以看到免費溫泉泡腳區。礁溪鄉有三個免費泡腳的溫泉公園，湯圍溝溫泉公園在礁溪鄉離火車站不遠處，就在大馬路邊，非常具有特色。整個公園很有設計感和實用感。很多遊客在逛公園時，就會忍不住脫下鞋泡泡腳。

Jiaohsi Hot Springs Park also offers free foot spas. In this park, the visitors can not only enjoy a foot spa, but they can rent bicycles to ride around Jaohsi. There are many good places to visit in Jaohsi, but parking is not convenient, making biking a good way to tour the area. The newest free foot spa park, with 4 free foot spas was built in 2012 and is called Jaohsi Hot Springs Plaza.

礁溪溫泉公園也有免費的足湯可以泡，這裡除了可以享受泡腳樂趣外、還可到遊客中心租借單車來逛礁溪，礁溪這有許多好玩的所在，可惜停車不方便，利用鐵馬來到處逛不止方便還可做運動。最新的免費泡腳公園是在 2012 時完成的， 名為礁溪溫泉地景廣場，除了有廣場整體設計外，這裡有提供四座免費泡腳池。

1 短獨白「影子跟讀」和填空練習

2 短獨白獨立演練和詳解

3 短獨白模擬試題

UNIT ⓱

礁溪溫泉公園

▶▶ 影子跟讀「短獨白填空」練習 🎧 MP3 017

除了前面的**「影子跟讀短獨白練習」**，現在試著在聽完對話後，完成下列填空練習，從中強化生活場景中常見的字彙以及拼字能力，答案的話請參照前面的獨白！

There are many hot spring water _____ near the _____ _____ station in Ilan. If you walk around town, you will see _____ free foot _____. There are three hot springs _____ in Jaohsi that offer a free foot spa. Tangweigou Park is near the _____ station in Jiaosi, right by the _____ road. It is a _____ park that is _____ to make visitors take off their shoes and ____ the water ____ the foot spas.

在宜蘭市區的火車站口附近就有很多溫泉自然湧出，礁溪鎮上繞一圈就可以看到免費溫泉泡腳區。礁溪鄉有三個免費泡腳的溫泉公園，湯圍溝溫泉公園在礁溪鄉離火車站不遠處，就在大馬路邊，非常具有特色。整個公園很有設計感和實用感。很多遊客在逛公園時，就會忍不住脫下鞋泡泡腳。

Jiaohsi Hot Springs Park also offers free foot spas. In this park, the visitors can not only _____ a foot spa, but they can _____ _____ to _____ around Jaohsi. There are many good places to visit in Jaohsi, but parking is not _____, making biking a good way to tour the area. The _____ free foot spa park, ____ 4 free foot spas was built ____ 2012 and is called Jaohsi Hot Springs Plaza.

礁溪溫泉公園也有免費的足湯可以泡，這裡除了可以享受泡腳樂趣外、還可到遊客中心租借單車來逛礁溪，礁溪這有許多好玩的所在，可惜停車不方便，利用鐵馬來到處逛不止方便還可做運動。最新的免費泡腳公園是在 2012 時完成的， 名為礁溪溫泉地景廣場，除了有廣場整體設計外，這裡有提供四座免費泡腳池。

拉拉山水蜜桃

▶ 影子跟讀「短獨白」練習 🎧 MP3 018

此篇為「影子跟讀短獨白練習」，規劃了由聽「短獨白」的shadowing練習，強化聽力專注力和掌握各個考點，現在就一起動身，開始聽「短獨白」！

If you're visiting Taoyuan in June or July, make sure you try Lalashan's famous peaches. They are incredibly sweet and juicy. While there, take a hike among the ancient cypress trees in the Lalashan Nature Reserves. The Sacred Tree Grove is full of natural red cypress trees that range in age from 500 years old to nearly 3,000. In the late autumn, the leaves change from green to red. It is very colorful and attractive. Only the 30 hectares that contain the ancient cypress grove are open to visitors while the rest of the reserve is set aside for ecological conservation.

當你在六月中至七月底去桃園玩，你一定要試試拉拉山出名的水蜜桃。拉拉山的水蜜桃香甜多汁。拉拉山自然保護區內有很多巨大的神木，其天然紅檜巨木林樹齡約在 500 年至 3,000 年

左右，每到深秋，園內變色植物由綠轉紅，五顏六色非常吸引人。拉拉山自然保護區並未全面開放遊客參觀，僅開放以神木群為主的地區約 30 公頃。

This area is an important ecological conservation area in Taiwan with many rare wild animals, such as the Formosan black bear, macaques, and muntjac deer. Bird watchers come here to spot the diverse and unique bird species.

拉拉山自然保護區內有很多難得一見的野生動物，如臺灣黑熊、彌猴、山羌等，是臺灣生態保育的重要地方，賞鳥者會到這裡來看種類繁多的獨特鳥類。

拉拉山水蜜桃

▶▶ 影子跟讀「短獨白填空」練習 🎧 MP3 018

　　除了前面的「**影子跟讀短獨白練習**」，現在試著在聽完對話後，完成下列填空練習，從中強化生活場景中常見的字彙以及拼字能力，答案的話請參照前面的獨白！

　　If you're _____ Taoyuan in _____ or July, make sure you try Lalashan's _____ _____. They are incredibly sweet and juicy. While there, take a hike among the ancient _____ trees in the Lalashan Nature _____. The Sacred Tree _____ is full ____ natural red cypress trees that _____ in age from 500 years old to nearly 3,000. In the late _____, the leaves _____ from _____ to _____. It is very _____ and _____. Only the 30 _____ that _____ the ancient cypress grove are _____ to visitors while the rest of the _____ is set ____ for _____ conservation.

　　當你在六月中至七月底去桃園玩，你一定要試試拉拉山出名的水蜜桃。拉拉山的水蜜桃香甜多汁。拉拉山自然保護區內有很

多巨大的神木,其天然紅檜巨木林樹齡約在 500 年至 3,000 年左右,每到深秋,園內變色植物由綠轉紅,五顏六色非常吸引人。拉拉山自然保護區並未全面開放遊客參觀,僅開放以神木群為主的地區約 30 公頃。

This area is an _____ ecological conservation area in Taiwan with many rare wild _____, such as the Formosan black _____, _____, and _____ _____. Bird _____ come here to spot the diverse and _____ bird species.

拉拉山自然保護區內有很多難得一見的野生動物,如臺灣黑熊、彌猴、山羌等,是臺灣生態保育的重要地方,賞鳥者會到這裡來看種類繁多的獨特鳥類。

UNIT ⑲

桃園－埔心牧場

此篇為「影子跟讀短獨白練習」，規劃了由聽「短獨白」的shadowing練習，強化聽力專注力和掌握各個考點，現在就一起動身，開始聽「短獨白」！

Are there really ranches, cows, and grassy fields in Taiwan? Yes, it's true, and it's just a one hour cab ride from downtown Taipei. Wei Chuan Pusin Ranch is located in Yangmei Township in Taoyuan County. Established in 1957, it was the first ranch in northern Taiwan. Originally a secluded woodland, over the years it's become a recreational tourist farm. Visitors of all ages can see farm animals in a natural setting. There are cows, lambs, ponies, and even Golden Pigs walking around.

牧場、牛和草原在臺灣，真的嗎？是的。從臺北市中心到這樣的地方坐計程車也才一個小時。這是位於桃園縣楊梅鎮的味全埔心牧場，這個牧場成立於1957 年也是北臺灣的第一座牧場。原本是偏僻林地，但是經過多年的開發，現在已經成為多功能的

觀光休閒牧場。不同年齡層的訪客可以在自然的環境看到農場動物。這個牧場裡有牛，有羊也有迷你馬，還有到處走的賽金豬。

The younger visitors will enjoy practicing their lassoing skills on wooden animals and the cowboy show is a must-see. Stay to enjoy the pig races and to watch the goats run an obstacle course. The Ecological Museum and Dairy Exhibition are good places for in-depth learning as they give talks on farming practices, past and present. Horse drawn carriage rides are available on weekends.

年紀較小的遊客可以對著木製動物練習丟套索技巧，牛仔表演也是不能錯過的，也可以欣賞豬的比賽，和看山羊跑障礙賽。這裡的生態體驗館和乳業展覽館是深入學習的好地方，因為他們會針對過去和現在的農場管理做主題演講。在週末時，可以搭乘馬拉的馬車到處逛。

桃園－埔心牧場

▶▶ 影子跟讀「短獨白填空」練習 🎧 MP3 019

除了前面的「**影子跟讀短獨白練習**」，現在試著在聽完對話後，完成下列填空練習，從中強化生活場景中常見的字彙以及拼字能力，答案的話請參照前面的獨白！

Are there really _____, _____, and grassy fields in Taiwan? Yes, it's true, and it's just a one hour _____ ride from _____ Taipei. Wei Chuan Pusin _____ is located _____ Yangmei Township in Taoyuan County. _____ in 1957, it was the first ranch in northern Taiwan. Originally a _____ _____, over the years it's become a _____ tourist farm. _____ of all ages can see farm animals _____ a natural setting. There are cows, _____, ponies, and even Golden Pigs walking around.

牧場、牛和草原在臺灣，真的嗎？是的。從臺北市中心到這樣的地方坐計程車也才一個小時。這是位於桃園縣楊梅鎮的味全埔心牧場，這個牧場成立於1957年也是北臺灣的第一座牧場。原本是偏僻林地，但是經過多年的開發，現在已經成為多功能的

觀光休閒牧場。不同年齡層的訪客可以在自然的環境看到農場動物。這個牧場裡有牛，有羊也有迷你馬，還有到處走的賽金豬。

The younger _____ will enjoy practicing their lassoing skills ____ wooden _____ and the _____ show is a must-see. Stay to enjoy the pig races and to watch the goats run an _____ course. The Ecological Museum and Dairy _____ are good places ____ in-depth _____ as they give talks on _____ _____, past and present. _____ drawn _____ rides are _____ on _____.

年紀較小的遊客可以對著木製動物練習丟套索技巧，牛仔表演也是不能錯過的，也可以欣賞豬的比賽，和看山羊跑障礙賽。這裡的生態體驗館和乳業展覽館是深入學習的好地方，因為他們會針對過去和現在的農場管理做主題演講。在週末時，可以搭乘馬拉的馬車到處逛。

苗栗-飛牛牧場

▶ 影子跟讀「短獨白」練習　🎧 MP3 020

　　此篇為**「影子跟讀短獨白練習」**，規劃了由聽**「短獨白」**的shadowing練習，強化聽力專注力和掌握各個考點，現在就一起動身，開始聽**「短獨白」**！

　　What do you get when you combine butterflies and milk cows? That would be the Flying Cow Ranch in Miaoli. With the motto of "no barrier between animals and humans", visitors interact with farm animals, wildlife, and butterflies up close. Adopt a lamb and take it for a walk, visit the butterfly sanctuary and see 10 different species, watch the frogs and the ducks in the ponds, and relax in the lush greenery and clean farm air. Plan on spending the night in clean and spacious rooms and enjoy indigenous recipes at one of the several restaurants.

　　想想如果能結合蝴蝶和乳牛會什麼的情景？那就是在苗栗的飛牛牧場。因為標榜「動物與人零距離」，所以遊客可以和農場動物，野生動物和蝴蝶做近距離互動。可以領一隻羊去散步，參

觀蝴蝶保護區，看看 10 個不同的品種，可以在池塘看青蛙和鴨子，也可以在青青草地上和乾淨的空氣放鬆心情。可以計劃在乾淨和寬敞的客房過夜，並去幾家餐館裡品嚐當地美食。

It's a place that combines a unique lifestyle with the ecological balance and commercial production. When it was commonly known as "Jiu Ceng Wo", the hillside was full of acacia trees. In 1975, the area was developed as the "Youth Dairy Ranch" and became a model professional dairy ranch in Taiwan. In 1985, the ranch was transformed into a recreational ranch. In 1995, it was officially opened to the public.

這裡是一個結合生態平衡及商業生產的地方，形成了相當獨特的生活方式。這裡原本是俗稱九層窩，是一片種滿相思樹林的山坡地。在 1975 年開墾為「中部青年酪農村」並成為臺灣的專業乳牛養殖示範區，1985 年轉型為休閒牧場。1995 年正式對外開放。

1 短獨白「影子跟讀」和填空練習

2 短獨白獨立演練和詳解

3 短獨白模擬試題

苗栗–飛牛牧場

▶▶ 影子跟讀「短獨白填空」練習　🎧 MP3 020

　　除了前面的「影子跟讀短獨白練習」，現在試著在聽完對話後，完成下列填空練習，從中強化生活場景中常見的字彙以及拼字能力，答案的話請參照前面的獨白！

　　What do you get when you _____ _____ and milk cows? That would be the Flying Cow Ranch in Miaoli. With the motto of "no barrier between animals and humans", visitors _____ _____ farm animals, _____, and butterflies up close. Adopt a _____b and take it for a walk, visit the butterfly _____ and see 10 _____ species, watch the _____ and the ducks in the_____, and relax in the _____ _____ and clean farm air. Plan on spending the night in clean and _____ rooms and enjoy _____ recipes _____ one of the several _____.

　　想想如果能結合蝴蝶和乳牛會什麼的情景？那就是在苗栗的飛牛牧場。因為標榜「動物與人零距離」，所以遊客可以和農場動物，野生動物和蝴蝶做近距離互動。可以領一隻羊去散步，參

觀蝴蝶保護區，看看 10 個不同的品種，可以在池塘看青蛙和鴨子，也可以在青青草地上和乾淨的空氣放鬆心情。可以計劃在乾淨和寬敞的客房過夜，並去幾家餐館裡品嚐當地美食。

It's a place that combines a unique _____ ____ the _____ balance and _____ _____. When it was _____ known as "Jiu Ceng Wo", the _____ was full of _____ trees. In 1975, the area was developed as the "Youth Dairy Ranch" and became a model _____ dairy ranch in Taiwan. In 1985, the ranch was _____ into a _____ ranch. In 1995, it was _____ opened to the _____.

這裡是一個結合生態平衡及商業生產的地方，形成了相當獨特的生活方式。這裡原本是俗稱九層窩，是一片種滿相思樹林的山坡地。在 1975 年開墾為「中部青年酪農村」並成為臺灣的專業乳牛養殖示範區，1985 年轉型為休閒牧場。1995 年正式對外開放。

UNIT ㉑

臺東－初鹿牧場

▶▶ 影子跟讀「短獨白」練習　🎧 MP3 021

　　此篇為**「影子跟讀短獨白練習」**，規劃了由聽**「短獨白」**的shadowing練習，強化聽力專注力和掌握各個考點，現在就一起動身，開始聽**「短獨白」**！

　　When you see cows spread across a vast green pasture with hay bales in the background, you probably think about European or American country life and not Taiwan. Many people can't believe that Taiwan has such a place. It is Chulu Ranch, which has about 72 hectares with 250 cows on it, near Taitung.

　　當你看到有乳牛分布在一片一望無際的綠油油牧草地，背景還有綑乾牧草時，你可能先想到的是歐洲或美國的鄉村生活而不是臺灣。很多人不敢相信臺灣也有這樣一個地方，這就是臺東的初鹿牧場，園區設立在臺東附近，面積約有72 公頃，飼養了250 頭乳牛。

　　Established in 1973, Chulu Ranch is only 18 km from

Taitung City. On a plateau at the altitude of 200-390 meters above sea level, it overlooks the Yuan Sen Applied Botanical Garden and the Pacific Ocean. Historically, this ranch is the oldest and largest ranch in the Taitung area with a grazing area, hay baling area, feeding area, and walkways inside the forest. A working dairy farm, 3.5 million kilogram cartons of milk are processed at the ranch yearly.

成立於 1973 年，初鹿牧場距離臺東市只有 18 公里，所在地是在海拔 200 至 390 公尺之間的高臺地上，俯瞰原生應用植物園及太平洋。初鹿牧場的這裡也是臺東地區歷史上最久遠的大型觀光牧場，牧場內規劃有放牧區、滾草區、餵食區、森林浴區等不同區域。這是一個乳製品農場，每年生產約 350 萬公斤的盒裝牛奶。

UNIT ㉑

臺東–初鹿牧場

▶▶ 影子跟讀「短獨白填空」練習 🎧 MP3 021

　　除了前面的**「影子跟讀短獨白練習」**，現在試著在聽完對話後，完成下列填空練習，從中強化生活場景中常見的字彙以及拼字能力，答案的話請參照前面的獨白！

　　When you see _____ spread across a vast green _____ with hay bales in the _____, you probably think about European or American _____ life and not Taiwan. Many people can't believe that Taiwan has such a place. It is Chulu _____, which has about 72 _____ with 250 cows on it, near Taitung.

　　當你看到有乳牛分布在一片一望無際的綠油油牧草地，背景還有綑乾牧草時，你可能先想到的是歐洲或美國的鄉村生活而不是臺灣。很多人不敢相信臺灣也有這樣一個地方，這就是臺東的初鹿牧場，園區設立在臺東附近，面積約有72 公頃，飼養了250 頭乳牛。

　　Established in 1973, Chulu Ranch is only 18 km _____

Taitung City. On a _____ at the _____ of 200-390 meters above sea level, it _____ the Yuan Sen Applied _____ Garden and the Pacific Ocean. _____, this ranch is the oldest and largest ranch ____ the Taitung area ____ a grazing area, hay baling area, feeding area, and _____ inside the forest. A working _____ farm, 3.5 million _____ _____ of milk are _____ at the ranch yearly.

成立於 1973 年，初鹿牧場距離臺東市只有 18 公里，所在地是在海拔 200 至 390 公尺之間的高臺地上，俯瞰原生應用植物園及太平洋。初鹿牧場的這裡也是臺東地區歷史上最久遠的大型觀光牧場，牧場內規劃有放牧區、滾草區、餵食區、森林浴區等不同區域。這是一個乳製品農場，每年生產約 350 萬公斤的盒裝牛奶。

花蓮民宿

▶ **影子跟讀「短獨白」練習** 🎧 MP3 022

此篇為**「影子跟讀短獨白練習」**，規劃了由聽**「短獨白」**的shadowing練習，強化聽力專注力和掌握各個考點，現在就一起動身，開始聽**「短獨白」**！

Slow down, unwind, and enjoy the view at the famous "Terrace Resort Hualien". The three European style buildings located 200 meters above the terraced hill in Shoufong Township in Hualien was a retirement dream for three friends living in the city. One of them renovated the old houses and in 2010 it began operation as a B&B. Many pieces of furniture in it were imported from Belgium and Germany.

慢下來，放輕鬆，好好地享受有名的「梯田山民宿」。這個有三棟歐式的建築就是有名的「梯田山民宿」，位在花蓮壽豐鄉 200 公尺高的梯田半山腰。這原本是三個築夢的城市人夢想在退休後在花蓮生活，其中一人就把原本在這裡的三戶老舊房屋重新改造，後來在 2010 年經營民宿。民宿裡的家具很多都是從比利時和德國採購的。

Even though the B&B is located in the middle of the mountains, without street lights, and the road is a small and narrow with steep inclines and curves, it is still a popular B&B. It has good online reviews because the B&B is well managed. There is no TV because the owner said there is no need for it since the view is so beautiful. Visitors should take the time to enjoy the slower pace of living here.

儘管這裡是山路、沒有路燈、羊腸小道、又陡又彎的地方，這家民宿還是非常受歡迎。因為用心的經營而有好的網路評價。這裡沒有電視，民宿主人說這麼美的景色不需要看電視，訪客應該要好好享受一下這邊的慢活步調。

1 短獨白「影子跟讀」和填空練習

2 短獨白獨立演練和詳解

3 短獨白模擬試題

花蓮民宿

▶▶ 影子跟讀「短獨白填空」練習 🎧 MP3 022

　　除了前面的**「影子跟讀短獨白練習」**，現在試著在聽完對話後，完成下列填空練習，從中強化生活場景中常見的字彙以及拼字能力，答案的話請參照前面的獨白！

　　Slow down, ＿＿＿＿, and ＿＿＿＿ the ＿＿＿＿ ＿＿＿＿ the famous "＿＿＿＿ Resort Hualien". The three ＿＿＿＿ style buildings located 200 meters above the ＿＿＿＿ hill in Shoufong ＿＿＿＿ in Hualien was a ＿＿＿＿ dream for three friends living in the city. One of them ＿＿＿＿ the old ＿＿＿＿ and in 2010 it began ＿＿＿＿ as a B&B. Many pieces of ＿＿＿＿ in it were ＿＿＿＿ from ＿＿＿＿ and ＿＿＿＿.

　　慢下來，放輕鬆，好好地享受有名的「梯田山民宿」。這個有三棟歐式的建築就是有名的「梯田山民宿」，位在花蓮壽豐鄉200 公尺高的梯田半山腰。這原本是三個築夢的城市人夢想在退休後在花蓮生活，其中一人就把原本在這裡的三戶老舊房屋重新改造，後來在 2010 年經營民宿。民宿裡的家具很多都是從比利時和德國採購的。

Even though the B&B is located _____ the middle of the _____, without street _____, and the _____ is a small and narrow _____ steep _____ and curves, it is still a popular B&B. It has good online reviews because the B&B is well _____. There is no TV because the owner said there is no need _____ it since the view is so _____. Visitors should take the time to enjoy the _____ _____ of living here.

儘管這裡是山路、沒有路燈、羊腸小道、又陡又彎的地方，這家民宿還是非常受歡迎。因為用心的經營而有好的網路評價。這裡沒有電視，民宿主人說這麼美的景色不需要看電視，訪客應該要好好享受一下這邊的慢活步調。

UNIT ㉓

南投民宿

▶ 影子跟讀「短獨白」練習　🎧 MP3 023

　　此篇為**「影子跟讀短獨白練習」**，規劃了由聽**「短獨白」**的shadowing練習，強化聽力專注力和掌握各個考點，現在就一起動身，開始聽**「短獨白」**！

　　Located at 1750 meters above sea level in Nantou, Chingjing Farm has a pleasant climate and beautiful scenery, so it attracts many tourists. However, there is a hidden crisis behind the beauty. The documentary *"Beyond Beauty - TAIWAN FROM ABOVE"* (2013) talks about the damage to the environment that is occurring in some of Taiwan's beautiful places. The harm done at Chingjing Farm encouraged public debate and forced Taiwan to examine the internal problems brought on by the development of tourist areas and the considerable impact on the environment and its ecosystems.

　　清境農場位在海拔 1750 公尺的南投，氣候宜人，景色優美所以吸引很多的觀光客。但是美麗的背後卻隱藏著危機。2013年發行的「看見臺灣」紀錄片，片中提到臺灣很多美麗地方的開

106

發，清境農場的環境傷害引起社會討論，也逼迫臺灣來檢視因觀光產業所帶來的內在問題，以及其對環境和生態系統相當大的影響。

The waste from daily water use, kitchen waste, and excess use of water from illegal B&Bs are part of the problem. However, the association of B&Bs in Chingjing Farm claim that they have a sustainability plan in place. Many B&B owners planted a large number of trees before the B&Bs were built. They also claim they will take responsibility for water and soil maintenance.

生活廢污水、廚餘垃圾、超量用水都突顯非法民宿的部分問題。但是，清境民宿業者自清說他們早有觀光產業永續發展概念，很多民宿在建屋前都會先在周邊種植大量樹木，也會負起水土保持的責任。

南投民宿

　　除了前面的「**影子跟讀短獨白練習**」，現在試著在聽完對話後，完成下列填空練習，從中強化生活場景中常見的字彙以及拼字能力，答案的話請參照前面的獨白！

　　Located at _____ _____ above sea level in _____, Chingjing Farm has a _____ climate and beautiful _____, so it attracts many tourists. However, there is a hidden crisis behind the beauty. The _____ *"Beyond Beauty - TAIWAN FROM ABOVE"* (2013) talks ____ the _____ to the _____ that is _____ in some of Taiwan's _____ places. The harm done at Chingjing Farm _____ public debate and forced Taiwan to _____ the _____ problems brought on by the _____ of tourist areas and the _____ impact on the _____ and its _____.

　　清境農場位在海拔 1750 公尺的南投，氣候宜人，景色優美所以吸引很多的觀光客。但是美麗的背後卻隱藏著危機。2013

年發行的「看見臺灣」紀錄片，片中提到臺灣很多美麗地方的開發，清境農場的環境傷害引起社會討論，也逼迫臺灣來檢視因觀光產業所帶來的內在問題，以及其對環境和生態系統相當大的影響。

The _____ from _____ water use, _____ waste, and excess use of water from _____ B&Bs are part ____ the problem. However, the _____ of B&Bs in Chingjing Farm _____ that they have a _____ plan in place. Many B&B owners planted a large number of trees before the B&Bs were _____. They also claim they will take _____ for water and soil _____.

生活廢污水、廚餘垃圾、超量用水都突顯非法民宿的部分問題。但是，清境民宿業者自清説他們早有觀光產業永續發展概念，很多民宿在建屋前都會先在周邊種植大量樹木，也會負起水土保持的責任。

宜蘭民宿

▶▶ 影子跟讀「短獨白」練習 🎧 **MP3 024**

此篇為**「影子跟讀短獨白練習」**，規劃了由聽**「短獨白」**的shadowing練習，強化聽力專注力和掌握各個考點，現在就一起動身，開始聽**「短獨白」**！

Any drama fan would jump at the chance to stay at the famous Kawoting B&B in I-Lan that was used in TWO dramas (*My Queen* with Ethan Ruan and Cheryl Yang and *The Happy Times That Year* with James Wen) as well as a Mitsubishi commercial. Built on a 1200 ping (1 ping equals 36 square feet) the orchard farm is on Snow Mountain. Surrounded by mountains, the stunning view overlooks the Lan Yang Plains. There is a total of eight unique rooms.

任何連續劇的戲迷都會抓住機會去住宜蘭的卡幄汀民宿，因為臺灣有兩部偶像劇都有在這個民宿拍攝，一部是阮經天和楊謹華主演的《敗犬女王》另一部是溫昇豪主演的《那一年的幸福時光》，還有一部三菱汽車廣告的場景也是在卡幄汀民宿。卡幄汀民宿建築在 1200 坪（1 坪等於 36 平方英尺）的果園之中，位

在海拔 100 公尺的雪山山脈下，三面環山一面俯瞰蘭陽平原的壯麗景色，總共有八個獨特形式的房間。

At check-in, the B&B owner provides homemade bamboo cakes and drinks. The owner's mother prepares a Chinese traditional breakfast with vegetables grown from her garden, homemade pickles, and pineapple flavored preserved tofu. The B&B also offers free afternoon tea time with coffee, tea, and pastries from 15:00 to 17:00 and has bikes you may borrow. It's difficult to find in the dark so take its phone number with you.

辦理入住手續的時候民宿主人會給提供自製的筍糕和飲品。傳統風味中式早餐是主人的母親煮的，會使用主人的母親自種的青菜及手工製作醬菜、豆腐乳等。民宿會在 15:00~17:00 免費提供有咖啡、果茶、糕點的下午茶，這裡也有可以借用的腳踏車。晚上路難找，所以要記得帶民宿的電話號碼。

宜蘭民宿

▶▶ 影子跟讀「短獨白填空」練習 🎧 MP3 024

除了前面的**「影子跟讀短獨白練習」**，現在試著在聽完對話後，完成下列填空練習，從中強化生活場景中常見的字彙以及拼字能力，答案的話請參照前面的獨白！

　　Any _____ fan would _____ ____ the chance to _____ at the famous Kawoting B&B in I-Lan that was used in TWO dramas (*My Queen* with Ethan Ruan and Cheryl Yang and *The Happy Times That Year* with James Wen) as well as a Mitsubishi _____. Built on a 1200 ping (1 ping _____ 36 square feet) the _____ _____ is on Snow Mountain. Surrounded by _____, the _____ view overlooks the Lan Yang Plains. There is a_____ of eight unique _____.

　　任何連續劇的戲迷都會抓住機會去住宜蘭的卡幄汀民宿，因為臺灣有兩部偶像劇都有在這個民宿拍攝，一部是阮經天和楊謹華主演的《敗犬女王》另一部是溫昇豪主演的《那一年的幸福時光》，還有一部三菱汽車廣告的場景也是在卡幄汀民宿。卡幄汀

民宿建築在 1200 坪（1 坪等於 36 平方英尺）的果園之中，位在海拔 100 公尺的雪山山脈下，三面環山一面俯瞰蘭陽平原的壯麗景色，總共有八個獨特形式的房間。

1 短獨白「影子跟讀」和填空練習

At check-in, the B&B owner _____ _____ _____ cakes and drinks. The owner's mother _____ a Chinese _____ breakfast ____ _____ grown from her _____, homemade _____, and _____ flavored _____ tofu. The B&B also offers free afternoon tea time ____ coffee, _____, and _____ from 15:00 to 17:00 and has bikes you may _____. It's _____ to find in the dark so take its _____ _____ with you.

2 短獨白獨立演練和詳解

辦理入住手續的時候民宿主人會給提供自製的筍糕和飲品。傳統風味中式早餐是主人的母親煮的，會使用主人的母親自種的青菜及手工製作醬菜、豆腐乳等。民宿會在 15:00~17:00 免費提供有咖啡、果茶、糕點的下午茶，這裡也有可以借用的腳踏車。晚上路難找，所以要記得帶民宿的電話號碼。

3 短獨白模擬試題

陽明山

▶▶ 影子跟讀「短獨白」練習　🎧 MP3 025

　　此篇為「影子跟讀短獨白練習」，規劃了由聽「短獨白」的shadowing練習，強化聽力專注力和掌握各個考點，現在就一起動身，開始聽「短獨白」！

　　Cows grazing in grassy fields near metropolitan Taipei? At Yangmingshan National Park, of course. Located on a volcanic terrain, geographically the park is part of the Datun Volcano area, so it's not a particular mountain.

　　在臺北大都會區附近，哪裡可以看到牛群吃牧草的情景？當然就在陽明山。陽明山國家公園的所在地是火山地形，在地理上是屬於大屯火山彙區域，所以陽明山並不是特定的山峰。

　　There are a lot of mountains and hills inside the Yangmingshan National Park. The third national park designated by the Taiwanese government, Yangmingshan Park is also known as the "Back Mountain Park" which is the best summer place in Taipei. Inside the Yangmingshan National Park there are parks, recreation areas, trails, ecological protected areas, and an educational center.

　　在這個區域裡有很多大山小山，後來被規劃為陽明山國家公園，是臺灣政府所設的第三個國家公園，陽明山公園又被稱為「後山公園」，是臺北地區最好的避暑地方。陽明山國家公園裡設有公園、遊憩區、步道、生態保護區和教育中心。

1 短獨白「影子跟讀」和填空練習

2 短獨白獨立演練和詳解

3 短獨白模擬試題

陽明山

▶▶ 影子跟讀「短獨白填空」練習 🎧 MP3 025

除了前面的「**影子跟讀短獨白練習**」，現在試著在聽完對話後，完成下列填空練習，從中強化生活場景中常見的字彙以及拼字能力，答案的話請參照前面的獨白！

Cows _____ in _____ fields near _____ Taipei? At Yangmingshan National Park, of course. _____ on a _____ _____, _____ the park is _____ of the Datun Volcano area, so it's not a _____ mountain.

在臺北大都會區附近，哪裡可以看到牛群吃牧草的情景？當然就在陽明山。陽明山國家公園的所在地是火山地形，在地理上是屬於大屯火山彙區域，所以陽明山並不是特定的山峰。

There are a lot of mountains and _____ inside the Yangmingshan _____ Park. The third national park _____ by the Taiwanese government, Yang-mingshan Park is also known _____ the "Back Mountain

Park" which is the best _____ place in Taipei. Inside the Yangmingshan National Park there are parks, recreation areas, _____, _____ _____ areas, and an _____ center.

在這個區域裡有很多大山小山，後來被規劃為陽明山國家公園，是臺灣政府所設的第三個國家公園，陽明山公園又被稱為「後山公園」，是臺北地區最好的避暑地方。陽明山國家公園裡設有公園、遊憩區、步道、生態保護區和教育中心。

太魯閣

▶ **影子跟讀「短獨白」練習** 🎧 MP3 026

此篇為**「影子跟讀短獨白練習」**，規劃了由聽**「短獨白」**的shadowing練習，強化聽力專注力和掌握各個考點，現在就一起動身，開始聽**「短獨白」**！

Taroko Gorge National Park with a multitude of gorges and cliffs is one of Taiwan's Eight Special Attractions. Inside the park, some organisms from the Ice Age still exist, such as the Hynobius formosanus (Taiwan salamander). Its name means "magnificent and beautiful" in the language of the Truku tribe, an indigenous people who reside here.

有綿延不斷的峽谷和斷崖的太魯閣國家公園是臺灣八景之一。國家公園的高山地帶還保留了許多自冰河時期以來就有的生物如山椒魚（臺灣蠑螈）。這裡原住民的太魯閣族語言所謂的太魯閣的意思是「壯麗和優美」。

Most visitors know that Taroko Gorge refers to the

section from Taroko to Tianxiang on the Central Cross-Island Highway, which is nearly 20 km of narrow canyon road. Starting from Taroko archway, the beauty is everywhere. The best part of Taroko Gorge is from the Eagle's Nest to the Mother Bridge because this section has cliffs, canyons, rolling tortuous and curvy tunnels, marble and other rock formations, and streams. Water rafting is a unique way to see the gorge.

大多數的遊客所知道的太魯閣峽谷是指中橫公路從太魯閣至天祥，這有將近 20 公里的峽谷路段。由太魯閣牌樓進入後，處處都是美景，峽谷愈來愈窄，燕子口到慈母橋這段為太魯閣的精華區，有峭壁、斷崖、峽谷、連綿曲折的山洞隧道、大理岩層和溪流等風光，園內共有 27 座大山、高山、尖山和群峰。泛舟是一種很獨特的方式來觀看峽谷。

UNIT ㉖

太魯閣

▶▶ 影子跟讀「短獨白填空」練習 🎧 MP3 026

除了前面的**「影子跟讀短獨白練習」**，現在試著在聽完對話後，完成下列填空練習，從中強化生活場景中常見的字彙以及拼字能力，答案的話請參照前面的獨白！

Taroko Gorge National Park with a _____ of _____ and _____ is one of Taiwan's Eight Special _____. Inside the park, some _____ from the _____ still _____, such as the Hynobius formosanus (Taiwan salamander). Its name means "_____ and beautiful" in the _____ of the Truku tribe, an _____ people who reside here.

有綿延不斷的峽谷和斷崖的太魯閣國家公園是臺灣八景之一。國家公園的高山地帶還保留了許多自冰河時期以來就有的生物如山椒魚（臺灣蠑螈）。這裡原住民的太魯閣族語言所謂的太魯閣的意思是「壯麗和優美」。

Most visitors know that Taroko Gorge refers _____

the _____ from Taroko to Tianxiang on the _____ Cross-Island Highway, which is nearly 20 km of _____ canyon road. Starting from Taroko _____, the _____ is everywhere. The best part of Taroko Gorge is from the Eagle's Nest to the Mother Bridge because this section has _____, _____, rolling tortuous and curvy _____, _____ and other _____ _____, and _____. Water _____ is a unique way ____ see the gorge.

　　大多數的遊客所知道的太魯閣峽谷是指中橫公路從太魯閣至天祥，這有將近 20 公里的峽谷路段。由太魯閣牌樓進入後，處處都是美景，峽谷愈來愈窄，燕子口到慈母橋這段為太魯閣的精華區，有峭壁、斷崖、峽谷、連綿曲折的山洞隧道、大理岩層和溪流等風光，園內共有 27 座大山、高山、尖山和群峰。泛舟是一種很獨特的方式來觀看峽谷。

日月潭

▶ **影子跟讀「短獨白」練習** 🎧 MP3 027

此篇為**「影子跟讀短獨白練習」**，規劃了由聽**「短獨白」**的shadowing練習，強化聽力專注力和掌握各個考點，現在就一起動身，開始聽**「短獨白」**！

Sun Moon Lake is located in central Taiwan in Yuchi, Nantou. It's 748 meters above sea level and is the only natural lake in Taiwan (as well as the largest body of water). Sun Moon Lake area is Taiwan's aborigine Shao Tribe's area and was first called Zintun in Shao language. In the recorded history, there have been several names for Sun Moon Lake such as: Dragon Lake, Lake Candidius, and Nin-Isivatan lake.

日月潭位於台灣中央的南投魚池鄉，海拔 748 公尺、是臺灣唯一的天然大湖（也是範圍最大的水域），日月潭也是臺灣原住民邵族的居住地，日月潭最早的稱呼是邵語稱為 Zintun，在歷史的記載裡日月潭也有被稱為龍湖、康德湖、林一西巴坦湖等名稱。

Sun Moon Lake is a basin due to changes in the earth's crust. The water accumulates all year inside the mountain lake. It's said that the east side of the lake resembles the sun while the west side resembles the moon. The Sun Moon Lake Scenic Area is not only beautiful but also has a pleasant climate. The average July temperature is higher than 22 degrees Celsius and is slightly lower than 15 degrees Celsius in January.

日月潭的盆地是因為地殼的變動形成的。這個高山湖泊也是因長久累積的水量而來的。據說，湖的東側看起來像太陽，而西側看起來像月亮。日月潭風景區不僅美麗，也有宜人的氣候。七月平均氣溫高於攝氏22 度，1 月則低於攝氏 15 度。

日月潭

▶▶ 影子跟讀「短獨白填空」練習 🎧 MP3 027

　　除了前面的「**影子跟讀短獨白練習**」，現在試著在聽完對話後，完成下列填空練習，從中強化生活場景中常見的字彙以及拼字能力，答案的話請參照前面的獨白！

　　Sun Moon _____ is located in _____ Taiwan in Yuchi, _____. It's 748 meters above sea level and is the only natural lake in Taiwan (as well as the _____ body of water). Sun Moon Lake area is Taiwan's _____ Shao Tribe's area and was first called Zintun in Shao _____. In the _____ history, there have been _____ names for Sun Moon Lake such as: Dragon Lake, Lake Candidius, and Nin-Isivatan lake.

　　日月潭位於台灣中央的南投魚池鄉，海拔 748 公尺、是臺灣唯一的天然大湖（也是範圍最大的水域），日月潭也是臺灣原住民邵族的居住地，日月潭最早的稱呼是邵語稱為 Zintun，在歷史的記載裡日月潭也有被稱為龍湖、康德湖、林一西巴坦湖等名稱。

Sun Moon Lake is a _____ due to _____ in the earth's _____. The water _____ all year inside the mountain lake. It's said that the east side of the lake resembles the sun while the west side _____ the moon. The Sun Moon Lake _____ Area is not only beautiful _____ also has _____ _____. The _____ July temperature is higher than 22 degrees _____ and is _____ lower than 15 degrees Celsius in _____.

日月潭的盆地是因為地殼的變動形成的。這個高山湖泊也是因長久累積的水量而來的。據說，湖的東側看起來像太陽，而西側看起來像月亮。日月潭風景區不僅美麗，也有宜人的氣候。七月平均氣溫高於攝氏22度，1月則低於攝氏15度。

林語堂紀念館

▶▶ 影子跟讀「短獨白」練習　🎧 MP3 028

　　此篇為「影子跟讀短獨白練習」，規劃了由聽「短獨白」的shadowing練習，強化聽力專注力和掌握各個考點，現在就一起動身，開始聽「短獨白」！

"This I conceive to be the chemical function of humor: to change the character of our thought." – *Lin Yutang, the Master of humo*r

　　Before Lin Yutang, there was no Chinese word for humor. A writer, scholar, inventor, philosopher, linguist, and an educator, Lin Yutang is the one who translated the word "humor" into Chinese at a time when China needed some humor desperately. He later became a famous humorist in Chinese society. Nominated in 1940 and 1950 for a Nobel Prize for Literature, Mr. Lin Yutang was very familiar with Western cultures and was an excellent writer in both English and Chinese languages.

「我認為幽默的化學作用就是改變我們思想的特質。」─幽默大師林語堂

在林語堂之前中文裡本來是沒有幽默一詞，林語堂是一名作家、學者、發明家、哲學家、語言學家和教育家。把英文 humor 翻成「幽默」的就是林語堂，那時華人社會正是非常需要幽默感，他後來成為華人裡有名的幽默大師， 也在 1940 年、1950 年被提名為諾貝爾文學獎候選人。林語堂先生熟悉中西文化，他是國內優秀的雙語作家之一。

He published 11 books in Chinese, 40 books in English, and wrote 9 translation books. Through his colloquial writing, Lin Yutang introduced traditional Chinese culture to the world. A lot of westerners learned about Chinese culture because of Lin Yutang's writings and have studied him in college classes.

他有十一部中文著作、四十部英文著作以及九部翻譯作品。林語堂將中國傳統文化以通俗白話的方式介紹給全世界，所以西方有不少人因林語堂而認識中國文化，也有很多人在大學裡研究林語堂。

林語堂紀念館

▶▶ 影子跟讀「短獨白填空」練習　🎧 MP3 028

除了前面的「**影子跟讀短獨白練習**」，現在試著在聽完對話後，完成下列填空練習，從中強化生活場景中常見的字彙以及拼字能力，答案的話請參照前面的獨白！

"This I _____ to be the _____ function of _____: to change the _____ of our thought." – *Lin Yutang, the Master of humor*

Before Lin Yutang, there was no Chinese word for _____. A writer, _____, inventor, _____, linguist, and an _____, Lin Yutang is the one who _____ the word "humor" into Chinese at a time when China needed some humor _____. He later became a famous humorist _____ Chinese _____. _____ in 1940 and 1950 for a _____ Prize for _____, Mr. Lin Yutang was very _____ with Western cultures and was an _____ writer in both English and Chinese languages.

「我認為幽默的化學作用就是改變我們思想的特質。」─幽默大師林語堂

在林語堂之前中文裡本來是沒有幽默一詞，林語堂是一名作家、學者、發明家、哲學家、語言學家和教育家。把英文 humor 翻成「幽默」的就是林語堂，那時華人社會正是非常需要幽默感，他後來成為華人裡有名的幽默大師， 也在 1940 年、1950 年被提名為諾貝爾文學獎候選人。林語堂先生熟悉中西文化，他是國內優秀的雙語作家之一。

He _____ 11 books in Chinese, 40 books in English, and wrote 9 translation books. Through his _____ writing, Lin Yutang introduced traditional Chinese _____ to the world. A lot of _____ learned ____ Chinese culture because of Lin Yutang's _____ and have studied him in _____ classes.

他有十一部中文著作、四十部英文著作以及九部翻譯作品。林語堂將中國傳統文化以通俗白話的方式介紹給全世界，所以西方有不少人因林語堂而認識中國文化，也有很多人在大學裡研究林語堂。

淡水紅毛城

▶▶ 影子跟讀「短獨白」練習 🎧 **MP3 029**

此篇為**「影子跟讀短獨白練習」**，規劃了由聽**「短獨白」**的shadowing練習，強化聽力專注力和掌握各個考點，現在就一起動身，開始聽**「短獨白」**！

If there is one place in Taiwan that has witnessed the various eras of foreign regimes, it's Fort Santo Domingo. When visitors walk into the "Red Hair Castle" (Fort Santo Domingo), it feels like time is stuck in the 17th century. In 1628, the Spaniards built "Santo Domingo" in Tamsui as military, political, trade, and missionary base.

如果在臺灣有一個地方可以見證到不同時代的外來政權，那就是紅毛城。走進紅毛城會讓人感到好像又回到十七世紀的世代，西班牙人於 1628 年在淡水蓋「聖多明哥」城，主要作為軍事、政治、貿易、傳教的根據地。

In 1642 the Dutch attacked northward at The Chicken Cage (now Keelung) and defeated the Spaniards. The Dutch then demolished the original castle, rebuilt it and called it "Anthony Castle", which is the origin of Fort Santo Domingo. Taiwanese at that time called Dutchmen the "Red Hair", so this is how the "Red Hair Castle" gets the name. It later became the location for the British Consulate. It's now a museum that's open Tuesday – Sunday, 9 am to 5 pm, with free admission.

1642 年荷蘭人北上進攻雞籠（今基隆），擊退西班牙人，後來重新改建城堡稱為「安東尼堡」，這就是淡水紅毛城的由來。當時臺灣人稱荷蘭人為「紅毛」，所以「紅毛城」由此得名，後來成為英國領事館。現在是一個博物館，開放時間是週二到週日，上午 9 時至下午 5 時，免費入場。

UNIT ㉙

淡水紅毛城

▶ 影子跟讀「短獨白填空」練習　🎧 MP3 029

　　除了前面的「**影子跟讀短獨白練習**」，現在試著在聽完對話後，完成下列填空練習，從中強化生活場景中常見的字彙以及拼字能力，答案的話請參照前面的獨白！

　　If there is one place in Taiwan that has _____ the various eras ____ foreign _____, it's Fort Santo Domingo. When visitors walk into the "Red Hair _____" (Fort Santo Domingo), it feels like time is stuck in the 17th century. In 1628, the Spaniards built "Santo Domingo" in Tamsui as _____, political, trade, and _____ base.

　　如果在臺灣有一個地方可以見證到不同時代的外來政權，那就是紅毛城。走進紅毛城會讓人感到好像又回到十七世紀的世代，西班牙人於 1628 年在淡水蓋「聖多明哥」城，主要作為軍事、政治、貿易、傳教的根據地。

　　In 1642 the _____ attacked _____ at The

Chicken Cage (now Keelung) and _____ the Span-iards. The Dutch then demolished the _____ castle, rebuilt it and called it "Anthony Castle", which is the or-igin of Fort Santo Domingo. Taiwanese _____ that time called _____ the "Red Hair", so this is how the "Red Hair Castle" gets the _____. It later became the _____ for the British _____. It's now a _____ that's open _____ – Sunday, 9 am to 5 pm, with free _____.

1642 年荷蘭人北上進攻雞籠（今基隆），擊退西班牙人，後來重新改建城堡稱為「安東尼堡」，這就是淡水紅毛城的由來。當時臺灣人稱荷蘭人為「紅毛」，所以「紅毛城」由此得名，後來成為英國領事館。現在是一個博物館，開放時間是週二到週日，上午 9 時至下午 5 時，免費入場。

東海路思義教堂

▶ 影子跟讀「短獨白」練習 🎧 MP3 030

　　此篇為「影子跟讀短獨白練習」，規劃了由聽「短獨白」的shadowing練習，強化聽力專注力和掌握各個考點，現在就一起動身，開始聽「短獨白」！

　　Founded in 1955, Tunghai University was the first private university in Taiwan and was a Christian school. It was located in a remote and inaccessible part of the Tatu Mountains in Taichung at the time. Pastor Henry W. Luce and the United States Board of Christianity thought the campus lacked a place for spiritual study and a place to worship so they built a chapel. The chapel's design was collaboration between Ieoh Ming Pei and Chen Chi-kwan.

　　東海大學創立在 1955 年是臺灣第一所私立大學，也是教會學校。所在地是在臺中市大肚山當時為地處偏遠，交通不便。亨利溫特斯路思義牧師(Mr. Henry W.Luce)和美國基督教聯合董事會覺得校園附近缺少靈修與禮拜集會場所，因此決定在校內建一座教堂，這座東海教堂是由貝聿銘及陳其寬擔任教堂設計及發展

工作。

I.M Pei is a Chinese-born architect called the master of modern architecture, while Chen Chi-kwan worked with a famous Bauhaus architect before moving to Taiwan to supervise the building of the chapel. Designed to withstand earthquakes and typhoons, the building's design is breathtaking. Completed in 1963, insiders know that the best view to see the "beauty of the curve" of the chapel is directly in front of it or within a forty-five degree angle.

華人建築師貝聿銘是現代建築大師,而陳其寬之前則是與有名的包豪斯建築師一起工作,他後來搬到臺灣監督東海路思義教堂。這所教堂有防震和防颱風的設計,該建築的設計讓人感到驚嘆。在 1963 年完工,內行人都知道,最能看到教堂的「曲線美」是要站在教堂的正前面或在從 45度角來看。

東海路思義教堂

▶ 影子跟讀「短獨白填空」練習 🎧 MP3 030

除了前面的**「影子跟讀短獨白練習」**，現在試著在聽完對話後，完成下列填空練習，從中強化生活場景中常見的字彙以及拼字能力，答案的話請參照前面的獨白！

_____ in 1955, Tunghai University was the first private _____ in Taiwan and was a _____ school. It was located _____ a remote and _____ part of the Tatu Mountains in Taichung at the time. Pastor Henry W. Luce and the United States Board of _____ thought the campus lacked a place for _____ study and a place to _____ so they built a chapel. The chapel's design was _____ between Ieoh Ming Pei and Chen Chi-kwan.

東海大學創立在 1955 年是臺灣第一所私立大學，也是教會學校。所在地是在臺中市大肚山當時為地處偏遠，交通不便。亨利溫特斯路思義牧師(Mr. Henry W.Luce)和美國基督教聯合董事會覺得校園附近缺少靈修與禮拜集會場所，因此決定在校內建一座教堂，這座東海教堂是由貝聿銘及陳其寬擔任教堂設計及發展

工作。

I.M Pei is a Chinese-born _____ called the master of _____ architecture, while Chen Chi-kwan worked _____ a _____ Bauhaus _____ before moving to Taiwan to _____ the building of the chapel. _____ to _____ earthquakes and _____, the building's design is _____. Completed in 1963, _____ know that the best view to see the "beauty of the _____" of the _____ is _____ in front _____ it or within a forty-five degree _____.

華人建築師貝聿銘是現代建築大師，而陳其寬之前則是與有名的包豪斯建築師一起工作，他後來搬到臺灣監督東海路思義教堂。這所教堂有防震和防颱風的設計，該建築的設計讓人感到驚嘆。在 1963 年完工，內行人都知道，最能看到教堂的「曲線美」是要站在教堂的正前面或在從 45度角來看。

臺南古城

▶▶ 影子跟讀「短獨白」練習 🎧 MP3 031

此篇為「影子跟讀短獨白練習」，規劃了由聽「短獨白」的shadowing練習，強化聽力專注力和掌握各個考點，現在就一起動身，開始聽「短獨白」！

It's not often that a duck keeper becomes emperor. Discontented with the Qing Dynasty in the 1720's, Zhu Yugi left duck keeping behind and became a rebel. His rebellion pushed the Qing soldiers back to the mainland and he was crowned Emperor of the Eternal Peace Era. His leadership didn't last long as the Qing soldiers regrouped, recaptured Tainan, and took Zhu Yigi back to Beijing for execution. But he left his heart behind and is still considered the Protector of Tainan. The walls to the city were built during this time and remains of the East and South gates mark the location of the old city. Tainan has seen its share of upheavals and rebellions since it is the oldest city in Taiwan and the first capital in Taiwan.

看守鴨的人變成皇帝是不常見的。在 1720 年代鴨母王朱一貴因為不滿清朝，後來就不管養鴨事業成為了叛軍。他的起事讓清兵退回大陸，接著他就被加冕為皇帝，年號永和。他的在位並沒有持續多久，因為清朝士兵重新收復臺南，並把朱一貴帶回北京處決。他留下的是他對臺南的愛，所以他到目前仍然被認為是臺南的保護者。城市的城牆就是在此期間建造的，所存留的東門及南門就變成是老城區的記號。臺南見證過動盪和叛亂，臺南是臺灣最古老的城市也是第一個首都。

Nicknamed "The Phoenix City" because Phoenix flowers can be seen everywhere in Tainan in spring and summer. Phoenix flower is a symbol representative of Tainan's ability to bounce back in history. Old Tainan is memorable.

臺南的綽號是「鳳凰城」，因為鳳凰花在臺南市的春天和夏天到處可看到，也是象徵臺南在歷史上的反彈能力，古都臺南是很令人難忘的。

臺南古城

▶▶ 影子跟讀「短獨白填空」練習 🎧 MP3 031

　　除了前面的「**影子跟讀短獨白練習**」，現在試著在聽完對話後，完成下列填空練習，從中強化生活場景中常見的字彙以及拼字能力，答案的話請參照前面的獨白！

　　It's not often that a _____ keeper becomes _____. _____ with the Qing _____ in the 1720's, Zhu Yugi left duck keeping behind and became a _____. His _____ pushed the Qing _____ back ____ the _____ and he was _____ Emperor of the Eternal Peace Era. His _____ didn't last long as the Qing soldiers _____, _____ Tainan, and took Zhu Yigi back to Beijing for _____. But he left his heart behind and is still _____ the Protector of Tainan. The walls to the city were built during this time and remains ____ the East and South _____ mark the _____ of the old city. Tainan has seen its share of _____ and _____ since it is the oldest city in Taiwan and the first _____ in Taiwan.

　　看守鴨的人變成皇帝是不常見的。在 1720 年代鴨母王朱一貴因為不滿清朝，後來就不管養鴨事業成為了叛軍。他的起事讓清兵退回大陸，接著他就被加冕為皇帝，年號永和。他的在位並沒有持續多久，因為清朝士兵重新收復臺南，並把朱一貴帶回北京處決。他留下的是他對臺南的愛，所以他到目前仍然被認為是臺南的保護者。城市的城牆就是在此期間建造的，所存留的東門及南門就變成是老城區的記號。臺南見證過動盪和叛亂，臺南是臺灣最古老的城市也是第一個首都。

　　_____ "The Phoenix City" because Phoenix _____ can be seen everywhere in Tainan in spring and _____. Phoenix flower is a symbol _____ of Tainan's _____ to bounce back in _____. Old Tainan is _____.

　　臺南的綽號是「鳳凰城」，因為鳳凰花在臺南市的春天和夏天到處可看到，也是象徵臺南在歷史上的反彈能力，古都臺南是很令人難忘的。

九份

▶ **影子跟讀「短獨白」練習** 🎧 **MP3 032**

　　此篇為「**影子跟讀短獨白練習**」，規劃了由聽「**短獨白**」的shadowing練習，強化聽力專注力和掌握各個考點，現在就一起動身，開始聽「**短獨白**」！

　　Jiufen, once a prosperous gold town during the Japanese occupation, seems untouched by time. The inspiration for *Miyazaki's Spirited Away* and the movie *City of Sadness*, the narrow cobblestone streets, rock walls, steep walkways, and Japanese tea houses feed the creative spirit. Stay until sunset and have a pot of tea in a tea house with a view of the water and mountains and pet the stray cats the town feeds.

　　九份這個城市曾在日本佔領臺灣期間是一個繁榮的金礦鎮，現在的九份似乎是一如既往。宮崎駿的神隱少女和悲情城市的靈感都是來自九份，狹窄的鵝卵石街道、石壁、陡峭的步道，以及日式茶館都是創意的來源。在這裏可以一直待到日落，也可以在茶館喝茶看看高山美景，和摸摸這個鎮裡所養的流浪貓。

This is the place to buy unique souvenirs as well. There are puppets with wooden display stands (like the street puppets you spot frequently), the ocarina store, a calligraphy artist, and if you walk to the end of the lane, there is an elderly man who engraves characters and images on black stones, while his wife strings them for you. They are memorable tokens of your visit. Come with images of your characters though since he doesn't speak English.

這也是購買獨特紀念品的地點。這裡有賣有木架的木偶（很像你經常會看到的街頭木偶），也有陶笛店和書法藝術家。如果你走到小巷的盡頭，有一個年長者會在黑色石頭上做文字和圖片的雕刻，他的妻子幫你包裝好。這樣就會是一個很難忘的紀念品。你可以自己帶文字讓他做雕刻，但是他不會説英語。

九份

▶▶ 影子跟讀「短獨白填空」練習 🎧 MP3 032

　　除了前面的「**影子跟讀短獨白練習**」，現在試著在聽完對話後，完成下列填空練習，從中強化生活場景中常見的字彙以及拼字能力，答案的話請參照前面的獨白！

　　Jiufen, once a _____ gold town _____ the Japanese _____, seems _____ by time. The _____ for *Miyazaki's Spirited Away* and the _____ *City of Sadness*, the _____ cobblestone streets, _____ walls, _____ walkways, and Japanese tea houses feed the _____ spirit. Stay until _____ and have a pot of tea in a tea house with a _____ of the water and mountains and pet the stray cats the town feeds.

　　九份這個城市曾在日本佔領臺灣期間是一個繁榮的金礦鎮，現在的九份似乎是一如既往。宮崎駿的神隱少女和悲情城市的靈感都是來自九份，狹窄的鵝卵石街道、石壁、陡峭的步道，以及日式茶館都是創意的來源。在這裏可以一直待到日落，也可以在茶館喝茶看看高山美景，和摸摸這個鎮裡所養的流浪貓。

This is the place to buy unique _____ as well. There are _____ with _____ display stands (like the street puppets you spot _____), the ocarina store, a _____ artist, and if you walk to the end of the _____, there is an _____ man who _____ characters and _____ on black stones, while his wife _____ them for you. They are _____ _____ of your visit. Come with images of your _____ though since he doesn't speak _____.

這也是購買獨特紀念品的地點。這裡有賣有木架的木偶（很像你經常會看到的街頭木偶），也有陶笛店和書法藝術家。如果你走到小巷的盡頭，有一個年長者會在黑色石頭上做文字和圖片的雕刻，他的妻子幫你包裝好。這樣就會是一個很難忘的紀念品。你可以自己帶文字讓他做雕刻，但是他不會說英語。

三義

▶ 影子跟讀「短獨白」練習　🎧 MP3 033

　　此篇為「**影子跟讀短獨白練習**」，規劃了由聽「**短獨白**」的shadowing練習，強化聽力專注力和掌握各個考點，現在就一起動身，開始聽「**短獨白**」！

　　Great art leaves you asking three questions: who are we, where are we from, and where are we going? It's not usual for a wood carver's sculpture to make you question yourself, but that's what makes Ju Ming's art masterful and moving. Ju Ming was born in Tongsiao Township in Miaoli County, Taiwan. Tongsiao Township is located next to Sanyi. Born the youngest of 11 to a poor family, Ju Ming learned early the necessity of respecting nature and doing your best.

　　看到偉大的藝術品會讓你想要問三個問題：我們是誰、我們是從哪裡來的還有我們要去哪裡？並不是每個木雕家的雕像作品都能讓你對自己問這些問題，而這就是朱銘的藝術高超動人的原因所在。朱銘出生在臺灣苗栗縣通霄鎮，通霄鎮的隔壁就是三義鄉。朱銘從小家境貧寒，是家裡 11 個孩子中最小的，朱銘在很

小的時候就學習尊重自然的必要性，也知道要把自己做到最好。

Apprenticed to the Master Sculptor, Lee Chin-Chua, at 15, he studied wood carving and sketching in order to advance his craft. After some successes and failures, Ju Ming realized he was an artist, not a businessman, and his focus on the spiritual nature of his art made him a Master artist.

他在 15 歲時當雕刻大師李金川的學徒，他研究木雕和人像素描是希望能讓自己的手藝更進步。在經歷了一些成功和失敗後，朱銘意識到他是一個藝術家而不是一個商人，後來他專注於藝術的精神本質才讓他成為藝術大師。

三義

▶ 影子跟讀「短獨白填空」練習 🎧 MP3 033

除了前面的**「影子跟讀短獨白練習」**，現在試著在聽完對話後，完成下列填空練習，從中強化生活場景中常見的字彙以及拼字能力，答案的話請參照前面的獨白！

　　Great art _____ you asking three questions: who are we, where are we from, and where are we going? It's not _____ for a wood carver's _____ to make you question yourself, but that's what makes Ju Ming's art masterful and moving. Ju Ming was born _____ Tongsiao Township in Miaoli County, Taiwan. Tongsiao Township is _____ next to Sanyi. Born the youngest of 11 to a poor _____, Ju Ming learned early the _____ of _____ nature and doing your best.

　　看到偉大的藝術品會讓你想要問三個問題：我們是誰、我們是從哪裡來的還有我們要去哪裡？並不是每個木雕家的雕像作品都能讓你對自己問這些問題，而這就是朱銘的藝術高超動人的原因所在。朱銘出生在臺灣苗栗縣通霄鎮，通霄鎮的隔壁就是三義

鄉。朱銘從小家境貧寒，是家裡 11 個孩子中最小的，朱銘在很小的時候就學習尊重自然的必要性，也知道要把自己做到最好。

_____ to the Master Sculptor, Lee Chin-Chua, at 15, he studied _____ carving and _____ in order to _____ his craft. After some _____ and failures, Ju Ming _____ he was an artist, not a _____, and his _____ on the _____ nature ____ his art made him a Master artist.

他在 15 歲時當雕刻大師李金川的學徒，他研究木雕和人像素描是希望能讓自己的手藝更進步。在經歷了一些成功和失敗後，朱銘意識到他是一個藝術家而不是一個商人，後來他專注於藝術的精神本質才讓他成為藝術大師。

UNIT ③④

冷水坑古道

▶▶ 影子跟讀「短獨白」練習 🎧 MP3 034

　　此篇為「影子跟讀短獨白練習」，規劃了由聽「短獨白」的shadowing練習，強化聽力專注力和掌握各個考點，現在就一起動身，開始聽「短獨白」！

　　The highest peak of Qixing Shan (7 Star Mountain) is 1,120 meters. It takes about 3 challenging hours to hike the 7 km trail from the southern slope to the northern slope. The south side of the mountain is sheltered from the damaging monsoons, while the North side is exposed to the winter monsoons and is affected by them.

　　七星山的最高峰是1120米。大約需要3個小時的挑戰時間，才有辦法完成從南坡走到北坡這一段總計有7公里的山路。山的南側可以擋住破壞性季風，而北側則是面對冬季季風，並會受到季風的影響。

　　The hiker travels over two mountain peaks, around

a fantasy lake teeming with wildlife, and may descend through fog with poor visibility. Stone benches along the path provide a place to rest and enjoy the stunning view of Taipei and the Northern coast. It goes from relatively level to steep descent making the entire hike difficult. Menghuan Pond is covered in fog year around giving it a mystical appearance earning it the name of "Fantasy Lake".

徒步旅行者會走過兩個山峰，也會走過夢幻式的湖泊，周圍也充滿野生動物，下坡時可能會遇到霧，能見度也較差。沿路都有石椅可以提供休息和享受臺北和北方海岸的壯麗景色。這條路徑從相對平坦的路到非常陡峭的地方，使得整個行走很困難。夢幻湖也是全年霧氣籠罩，也因為神秘的外觀而贏得「夢幻湖」之稱。

冷水坑古道

　　除了前面的**「影子跟讀短獨白練習」**，現在試著在聽完對話後，完成下列填空練習，從中強化生活場景中常見的字彙以及拼字能力，答案的話請參照前面的獨白！

　　The _____ peak of Qixing Shan (7 Star Mountain) is 1,120 meters. It takes about 3 challenging hours to _____ the 7 km _____ from the southern _____ to the northern slope. The south side ____ the mountain is _____ from the _____ _____, while the North side is exposed ____ the _____ monsoons and is _____ by them.

　　七星山的最高峰是1120米。大約需要3個小時的挑戰時間，才有辦法完成從南坡走到北坡這一段總計有7公里的山路。山的南側可以擋住破壞性季風，而北側則是面對冬季季風，並會受到季風的影響。

　　The hiker _____ over two mountain peaks,

around a _____ lake _____ with _____, and may _____ through fog with poor _____. Stone _____ along the path _____ a place to rest and enjoy the _____ view of Taipei and the Northern _____. It goes from _____ level to _____ descent making the entire hike _____. Menghuan Pond is covered ____ fog year around giving it a _____ _____ earning it the name of "Fantasy Lake".

徒步旅行者會走過兩個山峰，也會走過夢幻式的湖泊，周圍也充滿野生動物，下坡時可能會遇到霧，能見度也較差。沿路都有石椅可以提供休息和享受臺北和北方海岸的壯麗景色。這條路徑從相對平坦的路到非常陡峭的地方，使得整個行走很困難。夢幻湖也是全年霧氣籠罩，也因為神秘的外觀而贏得「夢幻湖」之稱。

草嶺古道

▶▶ 影子跟讀「短獨白」練習 🎧 MP3 035

　　此篇為**「影子跟讀短獨白練習」**，規劃了由聽**「短獨白」**的shadowing練習，強化聽力專注力和掌握各個考點，現在就一起動身，開始聽**「短獨白」**！

　　"Clouds obey dragons and winds obey tigers" is a Chinese saying meant for the northeast coast Caoling Trail (otherwise known as the Grass Ridge Ancient Trail). Regional Commander Liu Ming-deng encountered strong wind and fog during an inspection tour in 1867. He carved the character for tiger into a rock, hoping to tame the wind. If the weather is nice, the views along the hike are spectacular, especially in the fall when the area is covered in snow white blossoms. More than a romantic walk, it connects you to the past as you walk past the ruins of the Lu House, a famous stopping point for travelers that is long gone.

　　「雲從龍，風從虎」，是中文俗語中特別用來描述東北海岸的草嶺古道。臺灣總兵劉明燈在 1867 年考察期間時遇到強風和

大霧，他把老虎雕刻在石頭上（虎字碑），希望能馴服風。如果天氣是好的話，步道沿途的景觀是很壯觀的，尤其是在秋天時雪白花朵到處都是。除了是一條浪漫的步道外，在走盧宅的廢墟時，就好像與過去結合起來，這裡是以前著名的旅客商品買賣地方。

Thousands of feet have trodden the pathway over the years and while the informational plaques in Chinese and English hint of the history, the cut stone walkway can't talk. If only it could!

每年都會有上千的足跡踏過這個途徑，中文和英文資料看板裡透露出一絲絲歷史的軌跡，石砌的步道是無法説話，但是如果會説話的話則會述説歷史！

草嶺古道

▶ 影子跟讀「短獨白填空」練習 🎧 MP3 035

除了前面的**「影子跟讀短獨白練習」**，現在試著在聽完對話後，完成下列填空練習，從中強化生活場景中常見的字彙以及拼字能力，答案的話請參照前面的獨白！

"Clouds obey dragons and winds obey tigers" is a Chinese saying meant for the _____ coast Caoling Trail (otherwise _____ as the Grass Ridge Ancient Trail). Regional Commander Liu Ming-deng encountered strong _____ and _____ during an _____ tour in 1867. He _____ the character for _____ into a rock, hoping to _____ the wind. If the weather is nice, the views along the hike are _____, especially in the _____ when the area is covered ____ snow white _____. More than a _____ walk, it connects you to the past as you walk past the ruins of the Lu House, a famous stopping point for _____ that is long gone.

「雲從龍，風從虎」，是中文俗語中特別用來描述東北海岸

的草嶺古道。臺灣總兵劉明燈在 1867 年考察期間時遇到強風和大霧，他把老虎雕刻在石頭上（虎字碑），希望能馴服風。如果天氣是好的話，步道沿途的景觀是很壯觀的，尤其是在秋天時雪白花朵到處都是。除了是一條浪漫的步道外，在走盧宅的廢墟時，就好像與過去結合起來，這裡是以前著名的旅客商品買賣地方。

Thousands of _____ have trodden the _____ over the years and while the _____ plaques in Chinese and English hint ____ the history, the cut _____ walkway can't talk. If only it could!

每年都會有上千的足跡踏過這個途徑，中文和英文資料看板裡透露出一絲絲歷史的軌跡，石砌的步道是無法說話，但是如果會說話的話則會述說歷史！

能高古道

▶ 影子跟讀「短獨白」練習 🎧 MP3 036

此篇為**「影子跟讀短獨白練習」**，規劃了由聽**「短獨白」**的shadowing練習，強化聽力專注力和掌握各個考點，現在就一起動身，開始聽**「短獨白」**！

During the Japanese occupation of Taiwan, the new rulers found it difficult to control Taiwan's indigenous people. Considered wild and barbaric, they treated them like savages who needed assimilation. They disarmed hunting tribes and moved them to the plains to farm, and when that didn't work, they used military campaigns, isolation, containment, and finally eradication. Pushed to their limit, the Seediq rebelled and attacked the Japanese community, killing 134 people-women and children. The military retaliated and blood was shed on both sides.

在日本佔領臺灣時，新的統治者發現他們很難掌控臺灣的原住民。他們覺得原住民是狂野和野蠻的，所以他們對待原住民就用對待野蠻人的方式，也覺得原住民需要被同化。他們解除狩獵

部落的武裝，並把原住民遷到平原農場，當這種方式無效時，他們就用軍事行動、隔離、圍堵的方式對待原住民，最終以消滅原住民為目的。因為自己被推到極限，賽德克族反叛並襲擊日本社區，殺害134 名婦女和兒童。日本用軍事報復造成雙方流血。

Of the 1,200 Seediq involved in the Wushe Incident, 644 died, some committing suicide. After a second incident, Japan rethought their strategy and changed their attitudes towards the aboriginal people, treating them like equals deserving of respect. Warriors of the Rainbow: Seediq Bale is a 2011 Taiwanese film about this time period and is worth watching. Some of the events in the movie happened on the Nenggao trail.

參與霧社事件的 1200 名賽德克人中有 644 人死亡，有的是自殺。同樣的事件發生第二次後，日本重新思考他們的戰略，改變他們對原住民的態度，用尊重平等的態度來對待他們。賽德克‧巴萊是 2011 年發行的臺灣電影，描述的就是這段時期所發生的衝突，是部很值得看的電影。有一些在電影中的事件就發生在能高古道。

能高古道

除了前面的「**影子跟讀短獨白練習**」，現在試著在聽完對話後，完成下列填空練習，從中強化生活場景中常見的字彙以及拼字能力，答案的話請參照前面的獨白！

During the Japanese _____ of Taiwan, the new _____ found it difficult to _____ Taiwan's _____ people. Considered wild and _____, they treated them like _____ who needed _____. They _____ hunting _____ and moved them to the _____ to farm, and when that didn't work, they used military _____, _____, _____, and finally _____. Pushed to their limit, the Seediq rebelled and attacked the Japanese _____, killing 134 people- women and _____. The military _____ and blood was _____ ____ both _____.

在日本佔領臺灣時，新的統治者發現他們很難掌控臺灣的原住民。他們覺得原住民是狂野和野蠻的，所以他們對待原住民就用對待野蠻人的方式，也覺得原住民需要被同化。他們解除狩獵

部落的武裝，並把原住民遷到平原農場，當這種方式無效時，他們就用軍事行動、隔離、圍堵的方式對待原住民，最終以消滅原住民為目的。因為自己被推到極限，賽德克族反叛並襲擊日本社區，殺害134名婦女和兒童。日本用軍事報復造成雙方流血。

Of the 1,200 Seediq involved in the Wushe Incident, 644 died, some committing _____. ____ a second incident, Japan _____ their _____ and changed their _____ towards the aboriginal people, _____ them like equals _____ of _____. Warriors of the Rainbow: Seediq Bale is a 2011 Taiwanese _____ about this time _____ and is worth watching. Some of the _____ in the movie happened ____ the Nenggao trail.

參與霧社事件的 1200 名賽德克人中有 644 人死亡，有的是自殺。同樣的事件發生第二次後，日本重新思考他們的戰略，改變他們對原住民的態度，用尊重平等的態度來對待他們。賽德克‧巴萊是 2011 年發行的臺灣電影，描述的就是這段時期所發生的衝突，是部很值得看的電影。有一些在電影中的事件就發生在能高古道。

琉璃藝術

此篇為**「影子跟讀短獨白練習」**，規劃了由聽**「短獨白」**的shadowing練習，強化聽力專注力和掌握各個考點，現在就一起動身，開始聽**「短獨白」**！

    Yang, Huishan and Chang, Yi are the Taiwanese artists that made Liuli glass art popular. Yang, Huishan was an actress and Chang,Yi was a director. When they were working together on a movie, they were looking for a piece of crystal glass that represented the fragility and love found in the nature of love and life. However, all the crystal glass artwork in Taiwan back then was imported. Eventually, they decided to start Liuli artwork using a proprietary Chinese technique and Liuligongfang was created in Taiwan in 1987.

    在臺灣讓琉璃藝術家諭戶曉的第一號人物是楊惠珊和張毅。楊惠珊是演員，張毅是導演，當時因為拍電影而用水晶玻璃的藝術品來表現出生命和愛情本質的美麗與脆弱。但是他們當時在臺灣所找的水晶玻璃，全部是舶來品，後來他們決定投入做出華人

專有的琉璃藝術。琉璃工房在 1987 年誕生於臺灣。

Their works are now in well-known museums worldwide. They brought alive the art of the ancient glass work, and insisted on using "Liuli" as the direct English translation from Chinese in their marketing. The translation of "Liuli" not only reflects their adherence to the original concept but also helped the Chinese Liuli claim its place in the art world.

他們的作品現在被全世界很多知名博物館所珍藏,他們不僅帶動了古老的琉璃藝術,他們也堅持以英文直接翻譯的琉璃「Liuli」來行銷全世界,這樣的堅持也是反映了他們的原始理念,就是讓華人的琉璃藝術能在全世界的藝術裡占一席之地。

UNIT 37

琉璃藝術

▶▶ 影子跟讀「短獨白填空」練習　🎧 MP3 037

　　除了前面的「**影子跟讀短獨白練習**」，現在試著在聽完對話後，完成下列填空練習，從中強化生活場景中常見的字彙以及拼字能力，答案的話請參照前面的獨白！

　　Yang, Huishan and Chang, Yi are the Taiwanese _____ that made Liuli glass art _____. Yang, Huishan was an _____ and Chang,Yi was a _____. When they were working together on a _____, they were looking ____ a piece of _____ glass that _____ the _____ and love found ____ the _____ of love and life. However, all the crystal glass artwork in _____ back then was _____. Eventually, they _____ to start Liuli artwork using a _____ Chinese _____ and Liuligongfang was _____ in Taiwan in 1987.

　　在臺灣讓琉璃藝術家諭戶曉的第一號人物是楊惠珊和張毅。楊惠珊是演員，張毅是導演，當時因為拍電影而用水晶玻璃的藝術品來表現出生命和愛情本質的美麗與脆弱。但是他們當時在臺

灣所找的水晶玻璃，全部是舶來品，後來他們決定投入做出華人專有的琉璃藝術。琉璃工房在 1987 年誕生於臺灣。

Their works are now _____ well-known _____ worldwide. They brought _____ the art of the _____ glass work, and _____ on using "Liuli" as the direct English _____ from Chinese in their _____. The _____ of "Liuli" not only _____ their _____ to the original _____ but also helped the Chinese Liuli _____ its place in the art _____.

他們的作品現在被全世界很多知名博物館所珍藏，他們不僅帶動了古老的琉璃藝術， 他們也堅持以英文直接翻譯的琉璃「Liuli」來行銷全世界，這樣的堅持也是反映了他們的原始理念，就是讓華人的琉璃藝術能在全世界的藝術裡占一席之地。

鶯歌陶瓷

▶▶ **影子跟讀「短獨白」練習** 🎧 **MP3 038**

　　此篇為**「影子跟讀短獨白練習」**，規劃了由聽**「短獨白」**的shadowing練習，強化聽力專注力和掌握各個考點，現在就一起動身，開始聽**「短獨白」**！

　　If you plan on buying a tea set while visiting Taiwan, take a 30 minute train ride from Taipei and spend half a day exploring Yingge - a town known for its ceramics for 200 years. In the early days of Yingge, kilns and ceramic factories were everywhere. Known as "Taiwan's Ceramics City", it has nearly 200 ceramic shops on Yingge Ceramics Old Street, and has evolved into a tourist attraction with art studios and shops. Porcelain experts provide a large selection of unique items.

　　如果在臺灣旅遊的時候同時想要買茶具，你可以從臺北坐火車 30 分鐘到鶯歌以及花半天時間遊覽鶯歌，這是一個有 200 多年歷史的陶瓷小鎮，早期的鶯歌到處可以看到燒窯工廠和陶瓷工廠，這裡是臺灣的陶瓷重鎮，也被稱為「臺灣陶都」，鶯歌陶瓷老街有 200 家的陶瓷商店，這裡不只是陶瓷業的主要商業活動也

演變成觀光景點。這裡的瓷器專家會提供很多種購買的選擇。

The red brick buildings on the Old Street make people feel like they are walking back in time to the beginning of ceramics history. Old Street provides the complete pottery experience. The New Taipei City Yingge Ceramics Museum, near the Old Street, is the perfect place to learn about Taiwan's ceramics culture and history. In Yingge District, there are 24 walking trails leading to local temples.

老街上一長條都是紅磚建築讓人感受到走入陶瓷歷史的初期，在老街可以買陶、看陶也可以體驗作陶。新北市立鶯歌陶瓷博物館就在鶯歌老街附近，博物館可以讓遊客了解臺灣的燒窯文化和歷史。鶯歌區具有 24 條步道，其中很多步道可以走到不少廟宇。

鶯歌陶瓷

▶ 影子跟讀「短獨白填空」練習　🎧 MP3 038

　　除了前面的**「影子跟讀短獨白練習」**，現在試著在聽完對話後，完成下列填空練習，從中強化生活場景中常見的字彙以及拼字能力，答案的話請參照前面的獨白！

　　If you plan on buying a tea _____ while visiting Taiwan, take a 30 _____ train ride from Taipei and spend half a day _____ Yingge - a town known for its _____ for 200 years. In the early days of Yingge, kilns and ____ _____ were everywhere. Known as "Taiwan's Ceramics City", it has nearly 200 ceramic shops on Yingge Ceramics Old Street, and has _____ into a tourist _____ with art _____ and shops. Porcelain _____ provide a large _____ of ____ _____.

　　如果在臺灣旅遊的時候同時想要買茶具，你可以從臺北坐火車 30 分鐘到鶯歌以及花半天時間遊覽鶯歌，這是一個有 200 多年歷史的陶瓷小鎮，早期的鶯歌到處可以看到燒窯工廠和陶瓷工廠，這裡是臺灣的陶瓷重鎮，也被稱為「臺灣陶都」，鶯歌陶瓷

老街有 200 家的陶瓷商店，這裡不只是陶瓷業的主要商業活動也演變成觀光景點。這裡的瓷器專家會提供很多種購買的選擇。

The red _____ _____ on the Old Street make people feel like they are walking back in time to the _____ of ceramics _____. Old Street _____ the _____ _____ experience. The New Taipei City Yingge Ceramics Museum, near the Old Street, is the _____ place to learn about Taiwan's ceramics culture and history. In Yingge District, there are 24 walking _____ leading to local _____.

老街上一長條都是紅磚建築讓人感受到走入陶瓷歷史的初期，在老街可以買陶、看陶也可以體驗作陶。新北市立鶯歌陶瓷博物館就在鶯歌老街附近，博物館可以讓遊客了解臺灣的燒窯文化和歷史。鶯歌區具有 24 條步道，其中很多步道可以走到不少廟宇。

木雕

▶ 影子跟讀「短獨白」練習 🎧 MP3 039

　　此篇為**「影子跟讀短獨白練習」**，規劃了由聽**「短獨白」**的shadowing練習，強化聽力專注力和掌握各個考點，現在就一起動身，開始聽**「短獨白」**！

　　One famous Taiwanese wood crafter believes that his works show respect of nature and teach us that real beauty comes from following nature's way. Huang, Ma-Ching's classic woodwork that exemplifies his beliefs is a snail so realistic that viewers can see the slimy, soft skin of it. Born in 1952, in the fishing village of Lukang, he became a woodwork apprentice carving flowers, religious statues, and palanquins at the young age of 14. Later, he changed to a different artistic style that closer expressed his dedication to woodcarving.

　　有一個著名的臺灣木雕師認為，他的作品是要傳達我們要對大自然的尊重，真正的美就是順乎自然。黃媽慶最經典的蝸牛作品以其逼真到讓觀賞者可以看到蝸牛皮膚的黏滑和柔軟為他的信念作了最佳的示範。1952 年黃媽慶在鹿港北頭的漁村出生，十

四歲開始拜師學習刻花、神像、神轎雕刻，後來轉換不同的藝術路線來詮釋他對木雕的執著。

His exquisite techniques of carving the details of nature into wood are eye opening for many people. He prefers to use ordinary subjects to show his love of nature, such as common fruits, vegetables, insects, birds, and animals often seen in rural areas. He also expresses his concerns for the marine ecology and environmental conservation through his wood works.

在他細膩刀法下所刻劃出大自然的細節讓很多人大開眼界，他更喜歡用平凡無奇的題材來顯現他對大自然的熱愛，如農村常見的瓜果、蔬菜、昆蟲鳥獸，甚至會在作品中顯示出對海洋生態和環境保育的關心。

木雕

▶▶ 影子跟讀「短獨白填空」練習 🎧 MP3 039

除了前面的「**影子跟讀短獨白練習**」，現在試著在聽完對話後，完成下列填空練習，從中強化生活場景中常見的字彙以及拼字能力，答案的話請參照前面的獨白！

One famous Taiwanese wood crafter believes that his works show _____ of nature and _____ us that _____ beauty comes from following nature's way. Huang, Ma-Ching's classic _____ that _____ his _____ is a snail so _____ that viewers can see the slimy, soft skin of it. Born in 1952, in the fishing village of Lukang, he became a _____ _____ carving flowers, _____ statues, and pa-lanquins at the young age of 14. Later, he changed to a different artistic style that closer _____ his _____ to woodcarving.

有一個著名的臺灣木雕師認為，他的作品是要傳達我們要對大自然的尊重，真正的美就是順乎自然。黃媽慶最經典的蝸牛作品以其逼真到讓觀賞者可以看到蝸牛皮膚的黏滑和柔軟為他的信

念作了最佳的示範。1952 年黃媽慶在鹿港北頭的漁村出生，十四歲開始拜師學習刻花、神像、神轎雕刻，後來轉換不同的藝術路線來詮釋他對木雕的執著。

His _____ _____ of carving the _____ of nature into wood are eye opening for many people. He prefers to use ordinary subjects to show his love ____ nature, such as _____ fruits, _____, insects, birds, and animals often seen ____ _____ areas. He also expresses his _____ for the _____ ecology and _____ _____ through his _____ works.

在他細膩刀法下所刻劃出大自然的細節讓很多人大開眼界，他更喜歡用平凡無奇的題材來顯現他對大自然的熱愛，如農村常見的瓜果、蔬菜、昆蟲鳥獸，甚至會在作品中顯示出對海洋生態和環境保育的關心。

傳統書法

▶ 影子跟讀「短獨白」練習 🎧 MP3 040

　　此篇為「影子跟讀短獨白練習」，規劃了由聽「短獨白」的shadowing練習，強化聽力專注力和掌握各個考點，現在就一起動身，開始聽「短獨白」！

　　What goes into your heart and mind comes out on the paper in the high art form Shufa commonly called calligraphy. One of the 4 ancient disciplines of an educated person, it requires balance and control to master it. Since the middle of the 2nd century, calligraphy has been a critical part of the Chinese culture, often referred to as the flower of Chinese civilization. The director, Zhang Yimou, of the 2002 Hero interwove the art form into the storyline until it became a character as strong as the humans.

　　書法最高境界的藝術是可以表現出寫書法的人當時的心境。書法在古代對一個讀書人來說是要精通的四個學科之一，書法是需要平衡和控制才能精準的掌握書法。自第 2 世紀中以來，書法一直是中國文化的重要組成部分，通常被稱為中國文明之花。導

演張藝謀在 2002 年製作英雄這部電影，在電影裡導演用書法的藝術形式穿插在故事情節當中，並將其塑造成一個有如人一般的角色。

A student begins by copying exemplary works of a master until the copy is finally perfect. It may be copied thousands of times before it is deemed perfect. Each period of history has had its own forms, styles, and masters, and while people worry about it becoming a lost art, as long as people have characters to draw, it will continue on.

學習書法首先會從臨摹大師的字帖開始，直到臨摹到很完美為主。可能需要臨摹幾千次才會到達完美的程度。書法在每一個歷史時期都有不同的形式、風格和大師，當人們在擔心書法會成為一項失傳的藝術，其實只要中文字還是存在，書法就會繼續傳承。

1 短獨白「影子跟讀」和填空練習

2 短獨白獨立演練和詳解

3 短獨白模擬試題

傳統書法

▶ 影子跟讀「短獨白填空」練習 🎧 MP3 040

　　除了前面的**「影子跟讀短獨白練習」**，現在試著在聽完對話後，完成下列填空練習，從中強化生活場景中常見的字彙以及拼字能力，答案的話請參照前面的獨白！

　　What goes into your _____ and _____ comes out _____ the paper in the high art form Shufa _____ called _____. One of the 4 ancient _____ of an _____ person, it requires _____ and control to _____ it. Since the middle of the 2nd century, calligraphy has been a _____ part of the Chinese _____, often referred to as the flower of Chinese _____. The director, Zhang Yimou, of the 2002 Hero _____ the art form into the _____ until it became a _____ as _____ as the humans.

　　書法最高境界的藝術是可以表現出寫書法的人當時的心境。書法在古代對一個讀書人來說是要精通的四個學科之一，書法是需要平衡和控制才能精準的掌握書法。自第 2 世紀中以來，書法

一直是中國文化的重要組成部分，通常被稱為中國文明之花。導演張藝謀在 2002 年製作英雄這部電影，在電影裡導演用書法的藝術形式穿插在故事情節當中，並將其塑造成一個有如人一般的角色。

A student begins by _____ _____ works of a _____ until the copy is finally _____. It may be copied thousands of times before it is deemed perfect. Each period of history has had its own forms, _____, and masters, and while people _____ about it becoming a lost art, as long ____ people have _____ to draw, it will _____ on.

學習書法首先會從臨摹大師的字帖開始，直到臨摹到很完美為主。可能需要臨摹幾千次才會到達完美的程度。書法在每一個歷史時期都有不同的形式、風格和大師，當人們在擔心書法會成為一項失傳的藝術，其實只要中文字還是存在，書法就會繼續傳承。

UNIT 41

現代書法

▶ 影子跟讀「短獨白」練習 🎧 MP3 041

此篇為**「影子跟讀短獨白練習」**，規劃了由聽**「短獨白」**的shadowing練習，強化聽力專注力和掌握各個考點，現在就一起動身，開始聽**「短獨白」**！

When people compared Hsu Yung Chin's calligraphy to the famous master, Wang Xi-zhi, he knew he needed to do something different. He didn't want to be the next Wang Xi-zhi, but wanted his work to reflect his own feelings and thoughts. His belief that traditional calligraphy was disconnected from modern life led him to explore the concept of placing emotions over function. The founder of the avant garde calligraphy movement in Taiwan, Hsu Yung Chin transformed an ancient art form into something alive and full of feeling.

當自己的書法被拿來與名家大師王羲之相比時，徐永進就知道他需要做出不同的風格。他不想成為下一個王羲之，而是希望他的作品反映他自己的感受和想法。他認為傳統的書法和現代生活沒有聯結起來，因此促使他去探索如何把情緒擺在功能之上。

臺灣前衛風格的書法運動的創始人徐永進活生生把古老的藝術蛻變成充滿感情的作品。

His work continues to change as his perspective and life experiences change him. He may have changed the external form, but the internal form remains present. A modern master of the craft, he stuns people by the power, joy, and freedom he expresses. Spending time meditating and searching for the unity between nature and mind has shown fruit in his 2014 show, "The great square has no corners."

他的作品不斷地改變，正如他的看法和生活經歷改變他一樣。他可能是改變了外在形式，但內部形式仍然存在。就以這門藝術的現代大師來說，他用力量、快樂和自由的表現讓觀看者感到震撼。他花時間做沉思也會尋找自然與心靈之間的結合，這些都顯示在他的最新作品「大方無隅」。

現代書法

　　除了前面的**「影子跟讀短獨白練習」**，現在試著在聽完對話後，完成下列填空練習，從中強化生活場景中常見的字彙以及拼字能力，答案的話請參照前面的獨白！

　　When people compared Hsu Yung Chin's _____ to the famous master, Wang Xi-zhi, he knew he needed to do something _____. He didn't want to be the next Wang Xi-zhi, but wanted his work to reflect his own feelings and _____. His belief that _____ calligraphy was _____ from _____ life led him to _____ the _____ of placing _____ over _____. The founder of the avant garde calligraphy _____ in Taiwan, Hsu Yung Chin _____ an _____ art form into something alive and full ____ feeling.

　　當自己的書法被拿來與名家大師王羲之相比時，徐永進就知道他需要做出不同的風格。他不想成為下一個王羲之，而是希望他的作品反映他自己的感受和想法。他認為傳統的書法和現代生

活沒有聯結起來，因此促使他去探索如何把情緒擺在功能之上。臺灣前衛風格的書法運動的創始人徐永進活生生把古老的藝術蛻變成充滿感情的作品。

His work _____ to change as his _____ and life experiences change him. He may have changed the _____ form, but the _____ form remains _____. A modern master of the _____, he _____ people by the power, joy, and _____ he expresses. Spending time _____ and searching for the _____ between nature and mind has shown _____ in his 2014 show, "The great _____ has no _____."

他的作品不斷地改變，正如他的看法和生活經歷改變他一樣。他可能是改變了外在形式，但內部形式仍然存在。就以這門藝術的現代大師來說，他用力量、快樂和自由的表現讓觀看者感到震撼。他花時間做沉思也會尋找自然與心靈之間的結合，這些都顯示在他的最新作品「大方無隅」。

書法展覽

▶▶ 影子跟讀「短獨白」練習　🎧 MP3 042

此篇為**「影子跟讀短獨白練習」**，規劃了由聽**「短獨白」**的shadowing練習，強化聽力專注力和掌握各個考點，現在就一起動身，開始聽**「短獨白」**！

With the world facing major issues, such as environmental, socio-cultural, and ethical concerns, Taiwanese entrepreneur Dr. Yen- Liang Yin (Simon Yin) created the Tang Prize in 2012. Known as the Nobel Prize of Asia, the goal is to honor leaders who demonstrate original thought and make a major contribution to society regardless of nationality or ethnicity.

當整個世界都在面臨，如環境，社會文化和倫理的主要問題等時，臺灣企業家尹衍樑（西蒙‧尹）在 2012 年建立了唐獎。這被稱為亞洲的諾貝爾獎要頒發給不分國籍或種族，有創見思維和做出對社會重大貢獻的榮譽領導人。

The award goes to those doing first class research

in the fields of sustainable development, biopharmaceutical science, sinology (the academic study of China), and rule of law (the principle that law governs a nation and all its citizens- even the law makers). The prize laureates receive $40 million NT and another $10 million NT for research. In celebration of the awards, Taiwan spends the week of the Tang Prize celebrating and in 2014 the National Palace Museum organized a calligraphy exhibit from the Tang dynasty and the Song dynasty.

這個獎會頒給那些在可永續發展的生物製藥學，漢學（中國的學術研究），以及法治等領域（有關法律管治國家和所有公民的原則，甚至是立法者）做一流研究的人。獲獎者會獲得臺幣 $40,000,000 元和另外$10,000,000 元撥款作研究經費。為慶祝該獎項，每年在臺灣會有一個星期的唐獎週慶祝活動，在 2014 年時，則是在故宮博物院舉辦了唐朝和宋代的書法展覽。

1 短獨白「影子跟讀」和填空練習

2 短獨白獨立演練和詳解

3 短獨白模擬試題

書法展覽

▶ 影子跟讀「短獨白填空」練習 🎧 MP3 042

除了前面的「**影子跟讀短獨白練習**」，現在試著在聽完對話後，完成下列填空練習，從中強化生活場景中常見的字彙以及拼字能力，答案的話請參照前面的獨白！

With the world facing _____ issues, such as environmental, socio-cultural, and _____ concerns, Taiwanese entrepreneur Dr. Yen- Liang Yin (Simon Yin) created the Tang Prize in 2012. Known _____ the Nobel Prize of Asia, the _____ is to _____ leaders who _____ original thought and make a major _____ to society regardless of _____ or _____.

當整個世界都在面臨，如環境，社會文化和倫理的主要問題等時，臺灣企業家尹衍樑（西蒙‧尹）在 2012 年建立了唐獎。這被稱為亞洲的諾貝爾獎要頒發給不分國籍或種族，有創見思維和做出對社會重大貢獻的榮譽領導人。

The _____ goes to those doing first class

_____ in the fields of _____ _____, biophar-maceutical _____, sinology (the _____ study of China), and rule of law (the principle that law governs a nation and all its citizens- even the _____ makers). The _____ laureates _____ $40 million NT and another $10 million NT for _____. In _____ of the awards, Taiwan spends the week of the Tang Prize _____ and in 2014 the _____ Palace Museum _____ a calligraphy _____ from the Tang dynasty and the Song dynasty.

這個獎會頒給那些在可永續發展的生物製藥學，漢學（中國的學術研究），以及法治等領域（有關法律管治國家和所有公民的原則，甚至是立法者）做一流研究的人。獲獎者會獲得臺幣$40,000,000 元和另外$10,000,000 元撥款作研究經費。為慶祝該獎項，每年在臺灣會有一個星期的唐獎週慶祝活動，在2014 年時，則是在故宮博物院舉辦了唐朝和宋代的書法展覽。

元宵看天燈

▶ 影子跟讀「短獨白」練習 🎧 MP3 043

此篇為「**影子跟讀短獨白練習**」，規劃了由聽「**短獨白**」的shadowing練習，強化聽力專注力和掌握各個考點，現在就一起動身，開始聽「**短獨白**」！

Held on the first full moon of the Lunar New Year, the Lantern Festival symbolizes the arrival of spring. In a remote mountainous area, Pinghsi's sky lantern customs are over a hundred years old. In ancient times, the mountains were safe. However, bandits came to town during New Year's or festivals. The villagers hid in the mountains while the village keeper stayed behind.

元宵節是農曆新年的第一個月圓之夜，也象徵著春天的到來。平溪是在偏遠山區，放天燈的習俗有近百年的歷史。早期在山上的治安狀況良好，但是在年節或節慶還是會有盜匪出沒，村民只好躲避山中。

After the bandits left, the village keeper released a

sky lantern to inform the villagers that it was safe to come home. The day the villagers came home was on the 15th day of the Lunar New Year. It became a tradition for the people in Pinghsi to release sky lanterns (also called "The blessing light") to tell each other they are safe and sound. You can go there today and light your own sky lantern even if it's not the Lantern Festival.

留守的人在盜匪走後就在夜間放天燈作為信號讓山上避難的村民知道可以返家，當時他們返家日是農曆正月十五的元宵節，之後每年元宵節，平溪的村民就會放天燈來互報平安。因此天燈也稱為「祈福燈」。就算不是在元宵節，遊客在平時也可以到平溪放天燈。

元宵看天燈

▶▶ 影子跟讀「短獨白填空」練習　🎧 MP3 043

除了前面的「**影子跟讀短獨白練習**」，現在試著在聽完對話後，完成下列填空練習，從中強化生活場景中常見的字彙以及拼字能力，答案的話請參照前面的獨白！

　　Held on the first full _____ of the _____ New Year, the Lantern Festival _____ the _____ of spring. In a _____ _____ area, Pinghsi's sky _____ customs are _____ a hundred years old. In ancient times, the mountains were _____. However, _____ came to town during New Year's or _____. The _____ hid in the mountains while the _____ keeper stayed behind.

　　元宵節是農曆新年的第一個月圓之夜，也象徵著春天的到來。平溪是在偏遠山區，放天燈的習俗有近百年的歷史。早期在山上的治安狀況良好，但是在年節或節慶還是會有盜匪出沒，村民只好躲避山中。

After the _____ left, the village keeper _____ a sky lantern to _____ the villagers that it was safe to come home. The day the villagers came home was ____ the 15th day of the Lunar New Year. It became a _____ for the people in Pinghsi to release sky _____ (also called "The _____ light") to tell each other they are _____ and sound. You can go there today and _____ your own sky lantern even if it's not the Lantern _____.

留守的人在盜匪走後就在夜間放天燈作為信號讓山上避難的村民知道可以返家，當時他們返家日是農曆正月十五的元宵節，之後每年元宵節，平溪的村民就會放天燈來互報平安。因此天燈也稱為「祈福燈」。就算不是在元宵節，遊客在平時也可以到平溪放天燈。

UNIT 44

端午龍舟

▶ **影子跟讀「短獨白」練習** 🎧 **MP3 044**

此篇為**「影子跟讀短獨白練習」**，規劃了由聽**「短獨白」**的shadowing練習，強化聽力專注力和掌握各個考點，現在就一起動身，開始聽**「短獨白」**！

Politics were very messy during the period of the Warring states, and one man, Qu Yuan (a scholar, poet, statesman, and patriot), got caught in the middle between King Huai and lying ministers. Exiled, he spent his time researching local folktales, writing poetry, and mourning the state of his beloved country. When another warring state captured the capital, Qu Yuan drowned himself to demonstrate his sorrow. Upset, the villagers took to the river to save him, but they were too late.

戰國時期的政治相當的混亂，屈原（學者，詩人，政治家和愛國者）夾在楚懷王和官員之間。他後來在流亡時研究當地的民間故事，寫詩，悼念他深愛的國家。楚國為秦所滅，最後屈原在五月五日投江（汨羅江）自盡來證明自己的悲傷。村民們到河邊

要救他但已經太晚。

Beating on the drums, throwing rice in the river, and splashing the water with their paddles, they tried to save Qu Yuan from the dragon in the river. This practice continues today as the Dragon Boat Festival which commemorates Qu Yuan's sacrifice. Some people claim that it started as dragon worship and the Qu Yuan story happened later. Is the story real or a myth? Only the people from 2,000 years ago know for sure!

村民們敲著鼓，在河中扔糯米飯，划舟潑水試圖從在河裡的龍手中拯救屈原。現在端午節的習俗就是為了紀念屈原的犧牲。有些人聲稱，這一開始是表示對龍的崇拜，而屈原的故事是後來才發生的事情。這到底是真實的故事還是神話？只有 2,000 多年前的人才會知道事實的真相吧！

端午龍舟

▶ 影子跟讀「短獨白填空」練習 🎧 MP3 044

　　除了前面的「影子跟讀短獨白練習」，現在試著在聽完對話後，完成下列填空練習，從中強化生活場景中常見的字彙以及拼字能力，答案的話請參照前面的獨白！

　　_____ were very _____ during the period of the Warring states, and one man, Qu Yuan (a scholar, poet, statesman, and _____), got caught in the middle between King Huai and lying ministers. Exiled, he spent his time _____ local _____, writing _____, and mourning the state of his _____ country. When another warring state _____ the capital, Qu Yuan drowned himself to _____ his _____. Upset, the villagers took to the _____ to save him, but they were ____ late.

　　戰國時期的政治相當的混亂，屈原（學者，詩人，政治家和愛國者）夾在楚懷王和官員之間。他後來在流亡時研究當地的民間故事，寫詩，悼念他深愛的國家。楚國為秦所滅，最後屈原在五月五日投江（汨羅江）自盡來證明自己的悲傷。村民們到河邊

要救他但已經太晚。

Beating on the _____, throwing rice _____ the river, and _____ the water with their paddles, they tried to save Qu Yuan from the _____ in the river. This _____ continues today as the Dragon Boat Festival which _____ Qu Yuan's _____. Some people claim that it started _____ dragon _____ and the Qu Yuan story _____ later. Is the story real or a _____? Only the people from 2,000 years ago know for sure!

村民們敲著鼓，在河中扔糯米飯，划舟濺水試圖從在河裡的龍手中拯救屈原。現在端午節的習俗就是為了紀念屈原的犧牲。有些人聲稱，這一開始是表示對龍的崇拜，而屈原的故事是後來才發生的事情。這到底是真實的故事還是神話？只有 2,000 多年前的人才會知道事實的真相吧！

UNIT ⑮

中秋賞月

此篇為「影子跟讀短獨白練習」，規劃了由聽「短獨白」的shadowing練習，強化聽力專注力和掌握各個考點，現在就一起動身，開始聽「短獨白」！

If the smell of BBQ permeates Taipei's air and everyone is hanging out with family members and close friends around one, it must be the Mid- Autumn Festival. Also known as the August Moon Festival, it's Taiwan's harvest festival that occurs on the 15th day of the 8th lunar month (on the night of the full moon). The festival isn't a lavish lantern festival in Taiwan, like it is in Hong Kong or Singapore, but a time to gather, give thanks, and offer up prayers (very similar to the US's Thanksgiving).

如果燒烤的香味瀰漫臺北的空氣，每個人都與家庭成員和親密的朋友聚在一起，這個時候就是中秋節。每年農曆的八月十五（滿月的夜晚）好像是臺灣的豐年祭一樣。這個節日在臺灣不像在香港或新加坡是華麗的燈節，在臺灣的傳統是大家聚在一起，

表達感恩，並且拜神（非常類似美國的感恩節）。

It is a full moon, so it also means family reunion. Except in Taiwan, instead of turkey and dressing, they eat BBQ, moon cakes, and pomelos. Taipei has set up 11 riverside parks to help accommodate all the families wanting to BBQ outside.

這一天是滿月之日，象徵著團圓。但不是像美國用火雞加配料的傳統吃法，在臺灣大家是吃烤肉、月餅和柚子。臺北有設置 11 個河畔公園讓想在外面烤肉的家庭有地方可以烤肉。

中秋賞月

▶▶ 影子跟讀「短獨白填空」練習 🎧 MP3 045

除了前面的「**影子跟讀短獨白練習**」，現在試著在聽完對話後，完成下列填空練習，從中強化生活場景中常見的字彙以及拼字能力，答案的話請參照前面的獨白！

If the _____ of BBQ _____ Taipei's air and everyone is hanging out with family _____ and close friends around one, it must be the Mid- Autumn Festival. Also known as the August Moon Festival, it's Taiwan's harvest festival that _____ on the 15th day of the 8th lunar _____ (on the night ____ the full moon). The _____ isn't a _____ lantern festival in Taiwan, like it is in Hong Kong or _____, but a time to gather, ____ thanks, and offer up _____ (very similar to the US's _____).

如果燒烤的香味瀰漫臺北的空氣，每個人都與家庭成員和親密的朋友聚在一起，這個時候就是中秋節。每年農曆的八月十五（滿月的夜晚）好像是臺灣的豐年祭一樣。這個節日在臺灣不像在香港或新加坡是華麗的燈節，在臺灣的傳統是大家聚在一起，

表達感恩，並且拜神（非常類似美國的感恩節）。

It is a full _____, so it also means family _____. Except in Taiwan, instead of _____ and dressing, they eat BBQ, ____ cakes, and _____. Taipei has set up 11 _____ parks to help _____ all the families wanting ____ BBQ outside.

這一天是滿月之日，象徵著團圓。但不是像美國用火雞加配料的傳統吃法，在臺灣大家是吃烤肉、月餅和柚子。臺北有設置 11 個河畔公園讓想在外面烤肉的家庭有地方可以烤肉。

布袋戲

此篇為「**影子跟讀短獨白練習**」，規劃了由聽「**短獨白**」的shadowing練習，強化聽力專注力和掌握各個考點，現在就一起動身，開始聽「**短獨白**」！

The Bag Puppet" is a type of handheld puppet show which has a long history. "The Bag Puppet" got its name because the early puppet's body was just a bag made of cloth. The earliest puppetry was from China. For hundreds of years, "the Bag Puppet" was more popular in Taiwan when compared to other Chinese populated regions. The earlier puppet performer brought all the show objects in a case and stage boxes to the location where he was going to perform. He then easily set up the stage and performed.

布袋戲是歷史悠久的手操木偶戲，布袋戲的通稱是因為早期手操作戲偶的偶身只是用簡單像袋子的布料所做。布袋戲最早來自中國，幾百年後華人地區就以臺灣的發展最為蓬勃。布袋戲原來只是演出者肩擔戲箱與舞台到了定點後，簡易的搭起舞台，操

縱者就在布幃下演出戲台。

Later, Puppetry developed into professional groups. They performed on designated outdoor places then gradually they were invited to perform for the local gods. So outdoor puppetry can be seen in many temples in Taiwan. With the invention of the television, TV puppet shows appeared and later puppet shows on cable television, videos, movies, CDs, and multimedia.

後來布袋戲出現職業團體,也在指定地點做戶外野台戲,後來漸漸變成在廟宇前表演,所以臺灣很多廟宇在慶祝日時都可以看到戶外布袋戲。有了電視的發明後,也就出現了電視布袋戲,之後發展到有線電視、錄影帶、電影、光碟及多媒體。

布袋戲

除了前面的「**影子跟讀短獨白練習**」，現在試著在聽完對話後，完成下列填空練習，從中強化生活場景中常見的字彙以及拼字能力，答案的話請參照前面的獨白！

The Bag _____" is a type of _____ puppet _____ which has a long _____. "The Bag Puppet" got its name because the early puppet's body was just a bag made ____ _____. The earliest puppetry was from China. For hundreds of years, "the Bag Puppet" was more _____ in Taiwan when compared to other Chinese _____ regions. The earlier puppet _____ brought all the show _____ in a case and stage boxes to the _____ where he was going to _____. He then easily set up the _____ and performed.

　　布袋戲是歷史悠久的手操木偶戲，布袋戲的通稱是因為早期手操作戲偶的偶身只是用簡單像袋子的布料所做。布袋戲最早來自中國，幾百年後華人地區就以臺灣的發展最為蓬勃。布袋戲原

來只是演出者肩擔戲箱與舞台到了定點後，簡易的搭起舞台，操縱者就在布幃下演出戲台。

Later, Puppetry developed into _____ groups. They performed on _____ outdoor places then _____ they were _____ to perform for the local gods. So outdoor puppetry can be seen in many temples in Taiwan. With the _____ of the _____, TV puppet shows appeared and later puppet shows on _____ television, videos, movies, CDs, and _____.

後來布袋戲出現職業團體，也在指定地點做戶外野台戲，後來漸漸變成在廟宇前表演，所以臺灣很多廟宇在慶祝日時都可以看到戶外布袋戲。有了電視的發明後，也就出現了電視布袋戲，之後發展到有線電視、錄影帶、電影、光碟及多媒體。

藝術家

此篇為**「影子跟讀短獨白練習」**，規劃了由聽**「短獨白」**的shadowing練習，強化聽力專注力和掌握各個考點，現在就一起動身，開始聽**「短獨白」**！

In order to grasp the enormity of influence Lee Shih-chiao had on Taiwanese art; one needs a short history lesson. Until the 1890's, art was for religious use only and there were very few schools, so if you wanted to complete your education, you had to study elsewhere. As Taiwan became modernized, art schools began appearing, but an entire generation of artists had studied in Japan, France, and other places. Lee Shih-chiao was one of that generation. First in Japan and then in France, he learned his craft and the Western realistic style of work.

如果要了解李石樵對臺灣藝術的重大影響，我們先要知道一些相關的歷史。在1890 年之前，藝術在臺灣僅用於宗教用途，並僅有極少數的專門學校教授相關課程，所以如果你想完成你的

教育，你必須去其他國家學習。在臺灣慢慢現代化後，藝術學校開始出現，但在此之前，整整一代的藝術家都在日本，法國等地留學。李石樵就是這樣一代的人。他首先在日本，然後在法國，他學習手藝和西方寫實風格。

But the subjects closest to his heart were the people of Taiwan. His realistic works of Chinese subjects translated the Western art style and helped the Taiwanese people understand their value. Concerned about developing the next generation of artists who couldn't afford to study elsewhere, he co-founded the Taiyang Art Society and the Taiwan Art Exhibit which embraced young artists.

但是，在他內心最親近的主題是臺灣人。他用西方藝術風格表現出寫實的華人題材，他的作品幫助臺灣人了解自己的價值。他很關注下一代藝術家的養成，這些藝術家可能沒有財力支持他們去其他地方學習，他共同創辦了太陽藝術協會和臺灣藝術展鼓勵年輕藝術家的創作。

藝術家

▶▶ 影子跟讀「短獨白填空」練習 🎧 MP3 047

除了前面的**「影子跟讀短獨白練習」**，現在試著在聽完對話後，完成下列填空練習，從中強化生活場景中常見的字彙以及拼字能力，答案的話請參照前面的獨白！

In order to _____ the _____ of _____ Lee Shih-chiao had on Taiwanese art; one needs a ____ history lesson. Until the 1890's, art was for _____ use only and there were very few _____, so if you wanted to _____ your _____, you had to study elsewhere. As Taiwan became _____, art schools ____ appearing, but an _____ _____ of artists had studied in Japan, _____, and other places. Lee Shih-chiao was one ____ that generation. First in Japan and then in France, he learned his craft and the _____ realistic _____ of work.

如果要了解李石樵對臺灣藝術的重大影響，我們先要知道一些相關的歷史。在1890 年之前，藝術在臺灣僅用於宗教用途，並僅有極少數的專門學校教授相關課程，所以如果你想完成你的

教育，你必須去其他國家學習。在臺灣慢慢現代化後，藝術學校開始出現，但在此之前，整整一代的藝術家都在日本，法國等地留學。李石樵就是這樣一代的人。他首先在日本，然後在法國，他學習手藝和西方寫實風格。

But the _____ closest to his _____ were the people of Taiwan. His _____ works of Chinese subjects _____ the Western art style and helped the _____ people understand their value. Concerned _____ developing the next generation _____ artists who couldn't _____ to study elsewhere, he _____ the Taiyang Art Society and the Taiwan Art Exhibit which _____ young _____.

但是，在他內心最親近的主題是臺灣人。他用西方藝術風格表現出寫實的華人題材，他的作品幫助臺灣人了解自己的價值。他很關注下一代藝術家的養成，這些藝術家可能沒有財力支持他們去其他地方學習，他共同創辦了太陽藝術協會和臺灣藝術展鼓勵年輕藝術家的創作。

原住民音樂家

　　此篇為「影子跟讀短獨白練習」，規劃了由聽「短獨白」的shadowing練習，強化聽力專注力和掌握各個考點，現在就一起動身，開始聽「短獨白」！

　　Chen Da's hometown, Hengchun District, is at the entrance to Kenting National Park. It was featured in the movie, Cape No. 7, with the actors, Van Fan and Chie Tanaka, and local taxi driver will point out the movie's settings as he drives you to one of the many Kenting Resorts. Written and directed by Wei De-Shen, who also did The Seediq Bale, it remains the top grossing and prize winning film of the Taiwanese film industry. Hengchun Old Town is one of the best preserved historical towns with 4 intact gates and half of the walls still stand. While there, plan at least one day to be a beach bum. The brilliant blue waters and white sands look like a postcard, especially at sunset. Stay at a resort with beach access, so you can sleep with your windows open and fall asleep to the sound of crashing waves.

　　陳達的故鄉是在恆春，也是墾丁國家公園的入口處。這個地方出現在電影海角七號，演員有范逸臣與田中千繪，當地的計程車司機在開車帶你到處遊墾丁時經過這個地方也都會替遊客指出影片的場景。這部電影的編劇和導演是魏德聖，他也是電影賽德克巴萊的導演，這部片在臺灣電影界都有得到最高賣座和得獎。恆春古城是保存最完好的歷史名城之一，這裡有完整的四個大門，半面牆仍然站立著。當你在墾丁時，記得要計劃至少有一天去海灘逛逛。輝煌湛藍的海水和白色的沙灘看起來就像一張明信片，特別是在日落。住在海灘連接的度假飯店，這樣你可以在睡覺時打開你的窗戶，隨著海浪的聲音慢慢入睡。

原住民音樂家

除了前面的「**影子跟讀短獨白練習**」，現在試著在聽完對話後，完成下列填空練習，從中強化生活場景中常見的字彙以及拼字能力，答案的話請參照前面的獨白！

Chen Da's _____, Hengchun _____, is at the entrance to Kenting National Park. It was featured ____ the movie, ____ No. 7, ____ the actors, Van Fan and Chie Tanaka, and local taxi _____ will point ____ the movie's _____ as he drives you to one of the many _____ Resorts. Written and _____ by Wei De-Shen, who also did The Seedig Bale, it remains the top grossing and prize winning film of the Taiwanese film industry. Hengchun Old Town is one ____ the best _____ historical _____ ____ 4 intact gates and half of the walls still stand. While there, plan at least ____ day to be a beach bum. The _____ ____ waters and white sands look like a _____, especially at _____. Stay ____ a resort ____ beach _____, so you can sleep with your _____ open and fall asleep to the _____ of _____ waves.

　　陳達的故鄉是在恆春，也是墾丁國家公園的入口處。這個地方出現在電影海角七號，演員有范逸臣與田中千繪，當地的計程車司機在開車帶你到處遊墾丁時經過這個地方也都會替遊客指出影片的場景。這部電影的編劇和導演是魏德聖，他也是電影賽德克巴萊的導演，這部片在臺灣電影界都有得到最高賣座和得獎。恆春古城是保存最完好的歷史名城之一，這裡有完整的四個大門，半面牆仍然站立著。當你在墾丁時，記得要計劃至少有一天去海灘逛逛。輝煌湛藍的海水和白色的沙灘看起來就像一張明信片，特別是在日落。住在海灘連接的度假飯店，這樣你可以在睡覺時打開你的窗戶，隨著海浪的聲音慢慢入睡。

● 精選主題，側重解題思維和答題能
力，了解各種答題巧思後更能觸類
旁通，不會在寫完一堆題庫後，分
數仍卡在某個分數段，見樹不見林
般的失落，如欲演練更多試題可以
搭配《短獨白❶》書籍，學習成效
更為顯著。

Part

2

短獨白獨立
演練和詳解

Unit *1*
黑色購物節廣告：有 personal shopper 就不用感到迷失

🔍 Instructions

❶ 請播放音檔聽下列對話，並完成試題。 🎧 MP3 049

71. **Where might you hear this advertisement?**

    (A) a shopping mall

    (B) a Hello Kitty amusement park

    (C) a cartoon amusement park

    (D) a zoo

72. **According to this advertisement, what might personal shoppers do for consumers?**

    (A) renew membership

    (B) line up

    (C) go shopping

    (D) buying rabbits

73. **What does Black Friday imply in the advertisement?**

    (A) the day Jesus died

    (B) a major shopping day

    (C) the day before Christmas

    (D) Easter

聽力原文和對話

Questions 71-73 refer to the following advertisement

See the giant Hello Kitty and balloons of several cartoon characters...yep...it's Black Friday...Friddaaay. Come join us at our auction. For the first one hundred customers, there is a chance that you might get a renewed membership. For those whose shopping exceeds US 5000 dollars, you will be rewarded with line points and a gift bag. Also, we have our personal shoppers waiting for you. You won't feel that you are like a rabbit getting lost in the jungle...completely overwhelmed by tons of options. Tell our personal shoppers what you need... It's just that easy.

問題71-73請參閱下列廣告

看那巨大的Hello Kitty和幾個卡通人物的氣球...是的...這是黑色購物節...星期五五。加入我們的拍賣行列吧。前100位來訪的顧客，你可能有機會獲得更新的會員資格。對於那些購物超過5000美元者，我們會獎勵您line的點數和禮物袋。而且我們有我們的個人購物員等著你們。你不用感到你像隻在叢林中迷失的小白兔...對於許多選擇感到全然不知所措。告訴我們的個人購物員你需要的...就是這樣簡單。

答案：71. A 72. C 73. B

選項中譯和解析

71. 你可能在哪裡聽到這個廣告？

(A) 購物中心。

(B) Hello Kitty遊樂園。

(C) 卡通遊樂園。

(D) 動物園。

72. 依照此廣告，個人購物員可能替消費者做什麼？

(A) 更新會員資格。

(B) 排隊。

(C) 購物。

(D) 買兔子。

73. 在廣告中黑色星期五暗示什麼？

(A) 耶穌過世那天。

(B) 主要購物日。

(C) 聖誕節前一天。

(D) 復活節。

71.

‧ 此題詢問廣告地點，講者可能明白講述地點，也可能是使用較隱晦的表達，後者就會需要考生根據聽力訊息來進行推測。在試題變化中，出題者更進一步檢視考生是否有完全聽懂，而不是靠猜對的。**短獨白開頭的 Hello Kitty和cartoon characters就是陷阱**，綜合Black Friday和短獨白中段For those whose shopping exceeds US 5000 dollars...personal shoppers等線索，**推測答案是(A)** a shopping mall，而非(B) a Hello Kitty amusement park或(C) a cartoon amusement park。

72.

· 這題也是要區分所聽到的聽力訊息，**有些部分是聽力訊息中出現過的內容，但卻是干擾選項，不是題目問的**。根據短獨白最後一句Tell our personal shoppers what you need，告訴我們的個人購物員你需要的，言下之意，即消費者不用親自購物，個人購物員可以代勞，**故選(C)** go shopping。

73.

· 這題是推測題，廣告提到Black Friday之後，有auction拍賣，及shopping，personal shoppers等線索字，依這些線索字推測Black Friday主要跟shopping有關。

Unit 2
新聞報導：電腦小故障，但健身天氣播報男用海報代替

 **Instructions**

❶ 請播放音檔聽下列對話，並完成試題。 MP3 050

74. Which of the following is the closest to "a computer glitch"?
　　(A) a discount on computers
　　(B) a computer bug
　　(C) a poster shown on computer
　　(D) a weather forecast software

75. What kind of disaster will hit Florida during the weather forecast?
　　(A) a hurricane
　　(B) a typhoon
　　(C) a tornado
　　(D) an earthquake

76. Why does the weatherman say, "I guess people in Miami will feel so relieved..."?
　　(A) because the tornado might not strike Miami
　　(B) because people at Miami are quite used to tornadoes
　　(C) because people at Miami are already evacuated
　　(D) because people at Miami are not afraid of any disaster

聽力原文和對話

Questions 74-76 refer to the following news report

Good afternoon it's afternoon news. I can feel Florida heat even if I'm not outside. Let's see if an approaching tornado is gonna affect our weekend. There seems to be a computer glitch...our weatherman is trying to fix that...he certainly has been working out...

Weatherman: thanks...we do have a poster here...let me show you...see the tornado doubles its size when it reaches here...and it's getting bigger...it's gonna be the biggest in history...we're predicting two different routes...first it's gonna hit the Bahamas and land at Daytona and the second route would be directly landing at palm beach... no...not palm beach but cocoa beach...I guess people in Miami will feel so relieved...

問題74-76請參閱下列新聞報導

下午好這是下午新聞。我能感受到佛羅里達州的炎熱即使我不在外頭。讓我們看即將逼近的颶風是否影響我們周末。似乎有些電腦小故障...我們的天氣播報男正在修復...看來他確實有在健身...

天氣播報男：謝謝...我們這裡有海報...讓我們向你展示...看這颶風當它抵達這裡時體型成了雙倍...它漸漸增大...將會成為史上最大...我們正預測兩個不同路徑...第一個是他們會先侵襲巴哈馬然後於蝶同那登陸，而第二個路徑是它可能直接在棕櫚海灘..不...不是棕櫚海灘而是可可亞海灘登陸...我想在邁阿密的人會感到如釋重負。

答案：74. B 75. C 76. A

選項中譯和解析

74. 下列何者和「電腦小故障」的意思最接近?

　　(A) 電腦折扣。

　　(B) 電腦故障。

　　(C) 電腦顯示的海報。

　　(D) 氣象預報軟體。

75. 依照氣象預報,哪種災難將襲擊佛羅里達州?

　　(A) 颶風。

　　(B) 颱風。

　　(C) 龍捲風。

　　(D) 地震。

76. 氣象播報員為何說「我想在邁阿密的人會感到如釋重負」?

　　(A) 因為龍捲風可能不會襲擊邁阿密。

　　(B) 因為邁阿密的人們非常習慣龍捲風。

　　(C) 因為邁阿密的人們已經撤離了。

　　(D) 因為邁阿密的人們不害怕任何災難。

74.

‧這題是字彙和慣用語題。此題考computer glitch的類似字,glitch n.小毛病、小故障,講者提到a computer glitch的下一句也是解題線索:that our weatherman is trying to fix that。從fi,修理,一字能推測glitch有「故障」的意思。電腦故障的另一片語是**computer bug**,computer bug= computer glitch,故**要選(B)**。

75.

- 這題屬於細節題，能聽到相關細節或準確定位到就能答對，難度不高。此題問哪種災難將襲擊佛羅里達州，由短講提到的細節 see the tornado doubles its size when it reaches here，定位 tornado，颶風。

76.

- 這題難度較高，考驗考生的整合能力。這個題組包含了兩個講者，所以涵蓋的變化其實更多。從 I guess people in Miami will feel so relieved，「我想在邁阿密的人會感到如釋重負」是短講最後一句，因此回溯倒數第二句以推測氣象播報員這麼說的原因。倒數第二句：the second route would be directly landing at Palm Beach... no...not Palm Beach but Cocoa Beach，雖然沒有明說颶風路線不會襲擊邁阿密，但是可從 no...not Palm Beach（不會襲擊 Palm Beach）推測 Palm Beach 位於邁阿密，氣象播報員才會延續說「我想在邁阿密的人會感到如釋重負」。•

Unit **3**
動物園公告：鱷魚上演了大逃亡，但講者顯然把重點放在別地方了 XDD

🔍 Instructions

❶ 請播放音檔聽下列對話，並完成試題。 🎧 MP3 051

77. Why does the speaker say, "Oops...My office glass wall just shattered"?

(A) The glass was not bulletproof.

(B) The glass was shot by bullets.

(C) The police officers shot the glass.

(D) The glass was destroyed by the crocodiles.

78. What are the visitors told to do when they see the crocodiles?

(A) start panicking.

(B) remain calm.

(C) call the police.

(D) call animal specialists.

79. How is the weather on the day of this announcement?

(A) very hot

(B) warm

(C) very cold

(D) cool

聽力原文和對話

Questions 77-79 refer to the following announcement

Attention visitors! I do hope you enjoy your day in the zoo, and I'm here to inform you that our crocodiles seem to decide to have a day off or something. They're not in their compartments. But it's chilly out there. I'm not sure why they have to take a weekend getaway or something. I don't want you guys to panic. I've four animal specialists and police officers out there looking for them already. When you see them, just to keep calm...and you'll be fine...OMG what are they doing out there. Oops...My office glass wall just shattered. Apparently, I was fooled by Glass Company. It can't stand crocodile's punch.

問題77-79請參閱下列公告

觀光者們注意！我希望你們都能享受在動物園的時光，我在此是要告知你們我們的鱷魚們似乎決定想休息一天或幹嘛的。牠們不在我們的隔間裡。但是外頭相當寒冷。我不知道為什麼牠們想要上演個周末大逃亡或什麼的。我不想要你們感到驚嚇。我已經派四個動物專人和警察們找尋牠們。當你們看到牠們就保持冷靜...我想你們會沒事的...天啊牠們在這幹嘛...糟了...我的辦公司玻璃牆剛碎掉了。顯然我被玻璃公司騙了。它無法承受鱷魚的撞擊。

答案：77. D 78. B 79. C

77. 為何講者說「糟了...我的辦公司玻璃牆剛碎掉了」？

    (A) 玻璃牆不防彈。

    (B) 玻璃牆被子彈射擊。

    (C) 警官射擊玻璃牆。

    (D) 玻璃牆被鱷魚破壞了。

78. 訪客被告知看到鱷魚時該做什麼？

    (A) 開始驚慌。

    (B) 保持鎮定。

    (C) 打電話給警察。

    (D) 打電話給動物專家。

79. 在此宣布當天天氣如何？

    (A) 很熱。

    (B) 溫暖。

    (C) 很冷。

    (D) 涼爽。

77.

‧這題也是較具鑑別度的一題，要聽懂"Oops...My office glass wall just shattered"。綜合短講開頭描述「鱷魚們......不在我們的隔間裡」（our crocodiles ...... They're not in their compartments.）及考點句子的上一句:OMG what are they doing out there.，推測they指的是鱷魚，因此玻璃牆剛碎掉和鱷魚關係最密切，**故選(D)**。（還要注意的是，這是這個題組的短獨白末的訊息，但是卻擺在這個題組的第一題

出。）

78.

· 這題也是要小心的一題，根據When you see them, just to keep calm，知道講者告訴訪客保持鎮定。**故選(B)**。（但有些時候，卻因為很仔細聽講者的表達和情緒起伏，在選的時候誤選了其他選項，要注意區分「剛才有聽到講者說過」和「是否是題目所問的」。）

79.

· 此細節題詢問天氣，根據But it's chilly out there.，chilly，形容詞，寒冷的，**故選(C)**。（這題是剛開頭描述到快中段時的訊息，但卻擺在這個題組最後一題出，還有要注意的是，別憑感覺答題。）

Unit 4
廚房教學廣告：向您展示如何使用廚房器具，烤箱的去凍鍵就是好用啊！

🔍 Instructions

❶ 請播放音檔聽下列對話，並完成試題。 🎧 MP3 052

80. Where might you hear these instructions?

    (A) the turkey farm

    (B) a cooking school

    (C) a Thanksgiving party

    (D) a weapon store

81. Who might the speaker address?

    (A) gourmets

    (B) recipe writers

    (C) people interested in learning cooking

    (D) people interested in kitchenware

82. Why does the speaker say, "I'd like to show you my personal weapon...don't be afraid"?

    (A) He is trying to display his weapons.

    (B) He knows some people are scared by weapons.

    (C) When he says weapon, he's not referring to a real weapon.

    (D) He knows some people dislike guns.

聽力原文和對話

Questions 80-82 refer to the following instructions

Don't worry that you don't have any experience. Grab your apron and prepare all ingredients. Best kitchen will show you how. Before we start, I'd like to show you my personal weapon...don't be afraid..it's not a gun...it's a pot. It looks like it's new doesn't it, but I'm gonna tell you she is two years old...actually...it's been in use for 23 months...that's almost two years...see just a few scratches here...and really perfect for cooking fish and meat. I do have a really good oven ideal for cooking Thanksgiving turkey...let me demonstrate it for you. First defrost the turkey...see? Put it in the oven and press defrost...how convenient...

問題80-82請參閱下列操作說明

別擔心你不具備任何經驗。拿起你的圍裙和準備所有原料。倍斯特廚房將向你展示如何製作。在我們開始之前，我想要向你展示我的個人武器...別害怕...這不是槍...這是鍋具。這看起來像是新的，對不對?但是我要告訴你她兩年了...實際上，她已經使用了23個月...算成是使用兩年...看這裡只有幾個刮痕...拿來煮魚和肉品真的很完美。我有很好的烤箱，拿來煮感恩節的火雞會是很理想的廚具...讓我向你展示我第一個去凍火雞...看放進烤箱然後按「去凍」鍵...多方便啊!...。

答案：80. B 81. C 82. C

80. 你可能在哪裡會聽到這些指示？

    (A) 火雞農場。

    (B) 烹飪學校。

    (C) 感恩節派對。

    (D) 武器商店。

81. 講者可能是針對誰說話？

    (A) 美食家。

    (B) 食譜作家。

    (C) 對學習烹飪有興趣的人。

    (D) 對廚具有興趣的人。

82. 為何講者說「我想要向你展示我的個人武器...別害怕」？

    (A) 他正試著展示他的武器。

    (B) 他知道有些人害怕武器。

    (C) 當他說武器，他指的不是真的武器。

    (D) 他知道有些人不喜歡槍。

80.

· 依據Best kitchen will show you how.及let me demonstrate it for you，這兩句表達講者要給聽眾一些指示及示範，即講者的身份類似老師，所以**(B) a cooking school**最搭配此篇情境。

81.

· 綜合第10題的解題線索和第一句: Don't worry that you don't have

any experience，「別擔心你不具備任何經驗」。推測聽眾最可能的身份是學生，**最接近的選項是(C)**。

82.

· 這題也是要聽懂這個語境下所表達的意思。在題目考點句之後，講者馬上說: it's not a gun...it's a pot.，「這不是槍...這是大鍋」。可知他不是指真的武器，所以要選**選項(C)** When he says weapon, he's not referring to a real weapon.

Unit 5
新聞報導：遊樂園慈善親吻亭 ... 連播報員都要失守啦！

🔍 Instructions

❶ 請播放音檔聽下列對話，並完成試題。 🎧 MP3 053

83. **What do cheerleaders do in this activity?**

   (A) They perform gymnastics.

   (B) They donate money.

   (C) They give kisses.

   (D) They dance

84. **What is the main topic of the news report?**

   (A) a charity event

   (B) an amusement park

   (C) cheerleading

   (D) kissing skills

85. **Why does the speaker say, "Too bad, I'm a reporter"?**

   (A) He does not enjoy his job.

   (B) He does not think the quality of the report is excellent.

   (C) He thinks the charity is being held badly.

   (D) He cannot participate in the activity because of his identity.

聽力原文和對話

Questions 83-85 refer to the following news report

See the kissing booth over there...it's by far the greatest in Best amusement park. Every year there'll be numerous cheerleaders volunteering for this meaningful job. The money every guy pays goes totally to the charity. Too bad, I'm a reporter, or I will jump at the chance...they all look very gorgeous...there's a guy kissing a girl of my dreams...I can't watch it...there's another girl...seems she is sending me a mixed signal...come join us...even if it's a long line here...but you might be able to kiss your dream girl... this is Tim at Best amusement park.

問題83-85請參閱下列新聞報導

看親吻亭這裡...這是倍斯特遊樂園有史以來最盛大的。每年有許多啦啦隊員自願做這個有意義的工作。每個男子付的款項都會全部捐給慈善機構。真不巧我是記者，否則我會抓住這個好機會...她們看起來都很美麗...有個男子親了我夢想女孩...我無法再看下去了...又有另一個女孩...似乎她正向我遞送混雜的訊號...來加入我們吧!...即使這裡隊伍排的很長...但是你可能有機會能夠親到你夢想中的女孩...這是提姆於倍斯特遊樂園的報導。

答案：83. C 84. A 85. D

83. 在這場活動中啦啦隊員要做什麼？

(A) 他們表演體操。

(B) 他們捐錢。

(C) 他們親吻。

(D) 他們跳舞。

84. 此新聞報導主題為何？

(A) 慈善活動。

(B) 遊樂園。

(C) 啦啦隊活動。

(D) 親吻技巧。

85. 講者為何說「真不巧，我是記者」？

(A) 他不喜歡他的工作。

(B) 他不認為報導品質是優秀的。

(C) 他認為這場慈善活動舉辦得很糟。

(D) 因為他的身份他不能參與這場活動。

83.

· 第一句提到主題kissing booth，接著講者說: there'll be numerous cheerleaders volunteering for this meaningful job.和there's a guy kissing a girl of my dreams，綜合以上線索，推測啦啦隊員在這場活動中提供的是親吻服務，以志工的方式在親吻亭提供服務，所賺取的錢會用於慈善事業中，**故要選(C)** They give kisses.。

84.

・這題是詢問報導的主題，可以迅速定位到The money every guy pays goes totally to the charity.，尤其關鍵字charity，確定**正確選項是(A)**。選項(B) an amusement park和(C) cheerleading均是干擾選項，提供服務的是啦啦隊員沒錯，但是主題是這項活動，即慈善活動。

85.

・在題目考點句之後，講者馬上說: Too bad, I'm a reporter, or I will jump at the chance，「否則，我會抓住這好機會」，又考慮到考點句只表明他的身份是記者（其實他本身有心動而想參加），即不能參與的原因是因為其身份，因此**正確選項是(D)**。

Unit 6
購物網站廣告：家庭用品能魔法般出現在家門口喔！

 **Instructions**

❶ 請播放音檔聽下列對話，並完成試題。 MP3 054

86. Which of the following is the most likely to put on this advertisement?

    (A) tailors

    (B) an online shopping site

    (C) a diaper manufacturer

    (D) a convenience store

87. Why does the speaker quote this line, "The diapers just magically appear at our door"?

    (A) to show the high quality of the diapers

    (B) to advertise that they offer magic shows

    (C) to show how convenient the service is

    (D) to target consumers who need diapers

88. What kind of people is the most likely to use the service in this advertisement?

    (A) career women who have children

    (B) tailors

(C) single men

(D) young students

聽力原文和對話

Questions 86-88 refer to the following advertisement

Still struggling to balance your life and work...especially after giving birth to a second child...feeling so tired...and there seems to be a lot of chores waiting to be done. Just can't squeeze some time in to shop? Come to our website. We have all the specifically tailored household items for you. Let us do the magic for you. I'm quoting a most frequently used line from our customers. The diapers just magically appear at our door...it really is a great relief...don't hesitate to contact us...and we run 24/7. Just contact us.

問題86-88請參閱下列廣告

仍在平衡你的生活和工作中掙扎嗎？...特別是在生產第二個小孩過後...感到很疲憊嗎...而在這中間似乎有許多雜事等待你完成。就是無法擠出一些時間購物嗎？來我們的網站。我們有所有替您量身訂做的家庭用品。讓我們替您施展魔力吧。我來引述一個被我們顧客頻繁使用的台詞。尿布就像是魔法般地出現在我們家門口...這真的是讓人鬆一口氣...別猶豫聯絡我們...我們24小時都有營運，連絡我們就是了。

答案：86. B 87. C 88. A

1 短獨白「影子跟讀」和填空練習

2 短獨白獨立演練和詳解

3 短獨白模擬試題

選項中譯和解析

86. 下列何者最有可能刊登這則廣告？

(A) 裁縫師。

(B) 購物網站。

(C) 尿布製造商。

(D) 便利商店。

87. 為何講者引用這句「尿布就像是魔法般地出現在我們家門口」？

(A) 顯示尿布的高品質。

(B) 廣告他們有提供魔術表演。

(C) 顯示這項服務有多方便。

(D) 針對需要尿布的消費者。

88. 哪種人最有可能使用廣告裡的服務？

(A) 有小孩的職業婦女。

(B) 裁縫師。

(C) 單身男士。

(D) 年輕學生。

86.

· 這題是詢問「下列何者最有可能刊登這則廣告」，依據Just can't squeeze some time to shop? Come to our website.，推測此篇是購物網站的廣告，**故要選(B)** an online shopping site。（這題也是很明顯的給出了考點的訊息，有專注的聽，馬上對應到訊息就能選對。）

87.

・題目考點句之後，講者馬上說: it really is a great relief，真是讓人鬆一口氣，也可回溯短講開頭幾句都是描述聽眾在生活和工作中的辛苦，換言之此網站的服務讓聽眾的生活更方便，**故答案要選(C)** to show how convenient the service is，選項(B) to advertise that they offer magic shows和(D) to target consumers who need diapers均是干擾選項，magic shows和magically appear的音重疊，但不是表明會提供魔術表演，diapers的音也重疊，但是短獨白中所指的是購物者訂購尿布或物品，在運送方面對購物者來說會很方便，不是指標的客群是需要尿布的購物者。

88.

・這題是「哪種人最有可能使用廣告裡的服務」，詢問短獨白開頭幾句都是描述聽眾在生活和工作中的辛苦，尤其是especially after giving birth to a second child這句，especially這個副詞就暗示考生這句很重要，從此句推測**答案是(A)** career women who have children。

Unit 7
學院招生廣告：快來看看 go beyond that 指的是什麼呢？

🔍 Instructions

❶ 請播放音檔聽下列對話，並完成試題。 🎧 MP3 055

89. Which of the following is the closest to the word "spots" as in "we still have two spots left"?

    (A) dots
    (B) sightseeing spots
    (C) vacancies
    (D) spotlights

90. Why does the speaker mention that they are short of funds for their new computer lab?

    (A) to hold a fundraiser
    (B) to imply a way to draw applications
    (C) to ask for the donation of new computers
    (D) to ask for advice from parents

91. If parents want to ensure their children will be accepted by the Academy, what might they do?

    (A) They might talk to the principal directly.
    (B) They might train their children to have more talents.

(C) They might donate funds to the Academy.

(D) They might train their children to become bilingual.

1 短獨白「影子跟讀」和填空練習

聽力原文和對話

Questions 89-91 refer to the following line recordings

This is Linda...an admissions administrator of Best Academy...we still have two spots left. We're looking for kids with special talents. We will train them to outperform kids in other schools. We're welcoming kids with different backgrounds...like I always say we value diversity here at Best Academy...another thing that I would like to tell you is that we're short of funds for our new computer lab...so if anyone of you would like to go beyond that...I'll submit your paperwork directly to our principal...and there is an excellent chance...your kids might get far ahead of other candidates...you know how parents wanna send their kids to our school...

2 短獨白獨立演練和詳解

問題89-91請參閱下列line視頻

我是琳達...倍斯特學院的招生行政人員...我們仍有兩個空缺。我們在找尋有特別才能的小孩。我們會訓練他們到其能力勝過其他學校的小孩們。我們也歡迎不同背景的小孩...像是我總是說的，我們倍斯特學院這裡重視「多樣性」...另一件事我想讓你們知道的是我們對於新電腦實驗室仍資金短缺...所以如果你們任何人有想要做些超越那個的話...我會將您的書面作業直接遞給我們校長...有很大的機會是...你的小孩會比其他候選人都還前面...你知道父母有多想要將小孩送到我們學校...

3 短獨白模擬試題

答案：89. C 90. B 91. C

選項中譯和解析

89. 下列何者和「我們仍有兩個空缺」的「空缺」意思最接近？

   (A) 圓點。

   (B) 觀光景點。

   (C) 空缺。

   (D) 焦點。

90. 為何講者提到他們新的電腦教室資金不夠？

   (A) 為了舉辦募款會。

   (B) 暗示一種吸引申請案件的方式。

   (C) 要求捐新電腦。

   (D) 向家長徵詢建議。

91. 如果家長想確定他們的小孩能被學院接受，他們可能怎麼做？

   (A) 他們可能和校長直接談話。

   (B) 他們可能訓練小孩有更多才華。

   (C) 他們可能捐款給學院。

   (D) 他們可能訓練小孩會雙語。

89.

· 這題是字彙題，spot是多重意義字，因此一定要考慮題目考點句的情境，才能確定類似字。由第一句提及an admissions administrator of Best Academy，知道此篇是學校入學部門的宣佈，進而推測spot指的是「空缺」，**故要選(C)** vacancies。

90.

‧這題是詢問「為何講者提到他們新的電腦教室資金不夠」，講者提到「新電腦實驗室仍資金短缺」之後，馬上說「所以如果你們任何人有想要做些超越那個的...我會將你的書面作業直接遞給我們校長」，暗示家長可**透過捐款**，加快申請速度，即提供吸引申請案件的方式，**故要選(B)** to imply a way to draw applications。

91.

‧這題是詢問「如果家長想確定他們的小孩能被學院接受，他們可能怎麼做」，考慮第20題的線索句，講者暗示家長捐款，及your kids might get far ahead of other candidates的句意類似「家長想確定他們的小孩能被學院接受」，**故選(C)**。

Unit 8

談話：導遊在法國地窖的小小解說，可以嚐嚐白酒，但就別酒駕了

Instructions

❶ 請播放音檔聽下列對話，並完成試題。 MP3 056

92. **Who might the speaker be talking to?**
    (A) his father's friends
    (B) his family members
    (C) tourists
    (D) vintners

93. **Why does the speaker's father buy the cellar?**
    (A) to develop his hobby
    (B) for investment
    (C) to make more money
    (D) to store things he does not need

94. **What does "such a perfect blend" refer to?**

    (A) great taste of coffee
    (B) mixing cocktails
    (C) blending in the party
    (D) great taste of wine

聽力原文和對話

Questions 92-94 refer to the following talk

Welcome to our cellar. I'm your tour guide. My father bought this cellar in southern France a long time ago. This cellar mainly functions as a way to keep him from getting bored. As we all know about retirees...having nothing else to do but watch TV. He loves wine so one day it hit him...why not buy yourself a place where you can get to enjoy beautiful scenery and at the same time you can have time to do what you love...something you can only do when you retire. Have a taste of the chardonnay...such a perfect blend...just promise you won't drive after drinking...

問題92-94請參閱下列談話

歡迎來到我們的地窖。我是你們的導遊。我的父親在很久之前買下位於南法的地窖。這個地窖主要的功用是讓他免於無聊之苦。如同我們都知道關於所有退休者的生活…無所事事只能看看電視。他喜愛酒，所以有天他突然靈光一閃…想到為什麼不買個能讓你享受美麗風景且同時又能有時間做自己喜愛的事的地方呢？…一些你只能於退休後從事的事。…來嚐下夏多內白酒…如此完美的結合…答應我你不會在飲酒後開車。

答案：92. C 93. A 94. D

選項中譯和解析

92. 講者可能正向誰說話？

    (A) 他父親的朋友。

    (B) 他的家人。

    (C) 觀光客。

    (D) 酒商。

93. 為何講者的父親買酒窖？

    (A) 發展他的嗜好。

    (B) 為了投資。

    (C) 為了賺更多錢。

    (D) 為了儲藏他不需要的東西。

94.「如此完美的結合」指的是什麼？

    (A) 咖啡的美好滋味。

    (B) 調雞尾酒。

    (C) 在派對交際。

    (D) 酒的美好滋味。

92.

· 這題是詢問「講者可能正向誰說話」，這題是推測題，但是意思蠻明確的，所以難度不高，根據 I'm your tour guide.，馬上推測聽眾是觀光客**tourists**，故答案要選**C**。

93.

· 這題是詢問「為何講者的父親買酒窖」，根據This cellar mainly

functions as a way to keep him from getting bored.及you can have time to do what you love，推測當初購買酒窖的動機是發展喜歡的事物，換言之是**(A) to develop his hobby**。（這題很明確的表明了mainly functions，另外要能馬上將to do what you love對應到hobby）

94.

· 這題是詢問「如此完美的結合」的意思，根據such a perfect blend的前後文: Have a taste for the chardonnay及just promise you won't drive after drinking，確定考點片語指的是酒的完美味道，換言之是**(D) great taste of wine**。（這題如果了解blend的意思就能迅速攻略。）

Unit 9

百貨公司廣告：四個口紅口味，買超過還有精緻手提袋可以拿喔！

Instructions

❶ 請播放音檔聽下列對話，並完成試題。 MP3 057

95. According to the speaker, what is the effect of "a light brown shadow"?

(A) to highlight your eyes

(B) to reduce puffiness around the eyes

(C) to make you look thinner

(D) to make your skin darker

96. Why does the speaker mention "orange and grape flavors"?

(A) They are her favorite flavors.

(B) The auction provides desserts of orange and grape flavors.

(C) The company aims to sell more lipsticks of these two flavors.

(D) She does not wear lipsticks of these two flavors.

97. If a customer buys 6 lipsticks, what will she receive?

(A) free samples

(B) lipsticks of strawberry flavor

(C) lipsticks of grape flavor

(D) a beautiful handbag

聽力原文和對話

Questions 95-97 refer to the following advertisement

Hi everyone...Best cosmetics is having an annual auction. Try this. It really is perfect. A light brown shadow softens your puffiness. And our lipsticks. They have ten different flavors. See the shining color on my lip. It's orange flavor. I myself love the strawberry one...really sweet...but we're kind of promoting orange and grape flavors...so I picked orange. We're offering some samples for you, and with Christmas coming up, you can actually pick one as a present for your friends. We are gonna give customers purchasing more than four lipsticks an exquisite handbag.

問題95-97請參閱下列廣告

嗨，大家好...倍斯特化妝品將有年度販售。試試這個。這真的很完美。淡淡的棕色眼影柔和了你的眼袋。看我唇上的亮澤顏色。這是柳橙口味。我自己則喜歡草莓的...真的甜甜的...但是我們有點在推銷柳橙和葡萄口味...所以我選了柳橙口味的。我們將提供樣品給你們，隨著聖誕節的到來，你可以實際挑選一個當作禮物贈送給你的朋友們。我們會給購買超過四個口紅的顧客精緻的手提袋。

答案：95. B 96. C 97. D

95. 依據講者，「淡淡的棕色眼影」效果是什麼？

(A) 強調你的眼睛

(B) 減少眼周圍的浮腫

(C) 讓你看來更瘦

(D) 讓你的膚色更暗

96. 為何講者提到「柳橙和葡萄口味」？

(A) 它們是她最愛的口味。

(B) 拍賣會提供柳橙和葡萄口味的甜點。

(C) 公司的目標是賣更多這兩種口味的口紅。

(D) 她不塗這兩種口味的口紅。

97. 如果顧客買六支口紅，她會收到什麼？

(A) 免費樣品

(B) 草莓口味的口紅。

(C) 葡萄口味的口紅。

(D) 一個漂亮的手提袋。

95.

· 這題是詢問「淡淡的棕色眼影」的效果，能迅速理解字彙層面間的同義轉換就能馬上答對了，講者提到A light brown shadow的同一句，她說softens your puffiness，關鍵字puffiness是「浮腫」的名詞，**故答案要選(B)** to reduce puffiness around the eyes，其中softens your puffiness和reduce puffiness around the eyes兩者是同義轉換。

96.

· 這題是詢問為何講者提到「柳橙和葡萄口味」，依據we're kind of promoting orange and grape flavors，關鍵字promote，促銷，**換言之是(C)** 公司的目標是賣更多這兩種口味的口紅。

97.

· 這題是詢問「如果顧客買六支口紅，她會收到什麼」，依據最後一句：「購買超過四個口紅的顧客能得到精緻的手提袋」。 exquisite，精美的，**故選(D)** a beautiful handbag。（這題要注意的是，題目不一定會完全在數字等上頭與試題的表達一致，可能是包含在聽力訊息內，所以也是正確的選項，也有可能是超過某個數值，例如在題目中，買超過某個額度，所以也會對應到聽力訊息的最後一句的內容，能獲取的獎項。）

Unit 10
談話：遊樂園內部消息 透漏將有鬼屋的新增

Instructions

❶ 請播放音檔聽下列對話，並完成試題。 MP3 058

98. What does the speaker mean by "It's gonna wow you"?

(A) It will amaze you.

(B) It will frighten you.

(C) It will make you feel shocked.

(D) It will make you relaxed.

99. Where is this talk given?

(A) a castle

(B) a haunted house

(C) a cinema

(D) a department store

100. Which of the following is the closest to "It's just insider information"?

(A) information about movies

(B) the speaker's secret

(C) information not known to the public

(D) information about the new facilities

聽力原文和對話

Questions 98-100 refer to the following talk

Best cinema will be having a renovation from June 20 to July 28. We're really sorry for the inconvenience caused. Good news is that we are adding several facilities. It's gonna wow you when we reopen. I guess I'm gonna tell just a bit. For example, we are having a ghost castle. Whoever makes it to the end of the castle will get a free ticket, but whoever quits or not being able to make it to the end will get punished. It's just insider information...I hope I'm not revealing too much...

問題98-100請參閱下列談話

倍斯特電影將於6月20日到7月28日進行整修。我們對於所造成的不便感到抱歉。好消息是我們將新增幾項設施。當我們重新開張時您會因此而感到驚艷。我想我可以說一點點。例如，我們將有鬼屋城堡。只要是抵達城堡終點都將獲得免費的門票，但任何放棄或無法抵達終點的參加者將會受到懲罰。這只是內部消息...希望我沒有透露太多。

答案：98. A 99. C 100. C

選項中譯和解析

98. 講者說「它會讓你感到驚艷」的意思是什麼？

(A) 讓你感到神奇。

(B) 讓你害怕。

(C) 讓你驚嚇。

(D) 讓你放鬆。

99. 此短講在哪裡發生？

(A) 城堡。

(B) 鬼屋。

(C) 電影院。

(D) 百貨公司。

100. 下列何者和「這只是內部消息」意思最接近？

(A) 關於電影的資訊。

(B) 講者的秘密。

(C) 大眾不知道的資訊。

(D) 關於新設施的資訊。

98.

· 這題是詢問某個語句中的意思為何，看到題目可以迅速對應到選項中與該慣用語相同的意思，找到正確答案，It's gonna wow you是比較厘語的說法，wow由感嘆語轉換成動詞，指「讓人驚訝」，通常使用於正面情境，**(A) It will amaze you**最類似於It's gonna wow you的意思。（在寫聽力時，有些關鍵字就是解題關鍵，也是解題技巧之一，在這題中就要能迅速理解wow的意思，腦海中快速轉換到amaze。）

99.

・這題是典型的詢問地點的題目Where is this talk given，由開頭Best cinema馬上確定地點**(C)電影院**，注意雖然短講有提到a ghost castle，但(A) a castle和(B) a haunted house是陷阱選項，a ghost castle只是戲院的設備之一。（這題也是要在細節性訊息中，區分干擾選項，聽力理解力到位時，就能掌握核心重點，不會被其他旁枝末節干擾到。）

100.

・這題是慣用語題，insider information是慣用語，指「機密資訊」或「內部消息」。看到題目可以迅速對應到選項中與該慣用語相同的意思，找到正確答案，換言之是大眾不知道的資訊，**故選(C)**。

- 收錄更靈活且貼近實際生活情境的主題，並納入兩人對話更逼真的呈現天氣和新聞等話題，學習不枯燥，考生於寫完試題後，也可以仔細思考每個問題，並搭配解析觀看透徹了解出題者思維，並於考場中取得高分。

Part

3

短獨白模擬試題

聽力模擬試題

▶ PART 4 MP3 059

Directions: In this part, you will listen to several talks by one or two speakers. These talks will not be printed and will only be spoken one time. For each talk, you will be asked to answer three questions. Select the best response and mark the corresponding letter (A), (B), (C), (D) on your answer sheet.

71. Why does the man say, "a bit overshadowed by"?
(A) because he exaggerates the claim
(B) because he wants the flagstone as a gift from villagers
(C) because he thinks the flagstone actually prevails the company's expensive products
(D) because now he cannot cook faster

72. Why does the man want the camera to have a close-up?
(A) to make villagers jealous
(B) to impress the producer of the show
(C) to give photographers a genuine feel
(D) to highlight and promote the product

73. What distinguishes the food processor with villagers' knife?
(A) its engine
(B) its efficiency
(C) its price
(D) its weight

74. What is being advertised?
(A) the Chinese woks
(B) the dough with scallions
(C) fried water spinach
(D) the ladle

75. What aspect of the pan does the speaker applaud?
(A) the origin
(B) the light weight
(C) the heating part
(D) the shipment

76. Who most likely is the speaker addressing?
(A) housewives
(B) villagers
(C) executives of the kitchen wares
(D) the producer

77. What can be inferred about the merger?
(A) successful
(B) fruitful
(C) futile
(D) mysterious

78. Which of the following is closest in meaning to disintegrate?
(A) intact
(B) mystify
(C) consolidate
(D) dismiss

79. Why does the spokesperson say, "adds salt to injury"?
(A) To salvage the public image of the company
(B) to provide proof of the transferred money
(C) to refute the information from earlier news report

短獨白「影子跟讀」和填空練習 1

短獨白獨立演練和詳解 2

短獨白模擬試題 3

(D) to show that it makes the situation even worse

80. **According to the news report, what is the CEO getting accused of?**
    (A) forgery
    (B) murder
    (C) insider trading
    (D) corruption

81. **According to the news report, what can be found on a large ship?**
    (A) money
    (B) illegal documents
    (C) cruise
    (D) corpse

82. **Where is the news report given?**
    (A) Egypt
    (B) Europe
    (C) America
    (D) Asia

83. **Which of the following item is not instantly-lit in the fire accident?**
    (A) inflammable items
    (B) furniture
    (C) plastics
    (D) clothes

84. **What is mentioned about the firefighters?**
    (A) they are able to tackle the explosion
    (B) they are forced to leave the house
    (C) they demand more help
    (D) they don't have the authority to use helicopters

85.Which of the following was ravaged by the forest fire?
   (A) beasts
   (B) helicopters
   (C) firefighters
   (D)local inhabitants

86.What is unique about the Best Jewelry at the exhibition?
   (A)its comparatively low price
   (B) its durability
   (C) its design
   (D)its debut

87.Why does the speaker mention "don't worry that if you have a spouse that is not a local here"?
   (A)to enhance the authenticity of the jewelry
   (B) to demonstrate the credibility of the company
   (C) to clear the doubts
   (D)to make sure everyone will get the ticket

88.Which of the following will not be showcased in the approaching exhibition?
   (A)silver
   (B) gold
   (C) pearls
   (D)blue-like gems

89.Where most likely are the listeners?
   (A)at an annual auction
   (B) at the precious metal exhibition
   (C) at the jewelry processing plant
   (D)at the interpreter training center

90. **Which of the following could be about to be served?**
    (A) mini-burgers
    (B) chicken-wings
    (C) candy apple
    (D) wine

91. **What field does the speaker work in?**
    (A) jewelry design
    (B) cuisine catering
    (C) music industry
    (D) journalism

92. **What can be inferred about the weather before the typhoon?**
    (A) cloudy and with different types of clouds
    (B) clear
    (C) windy
    (D) rainy

93. **According to the weather man, where did the typhoon gather the most strength?**
    (A) at Korea
    (B) at Japan
    (C) at Guam
    (D) at the Philippines

94. **If the prediction of the typhoon goes as the international news, where will the typhoon first strike?**
    (A) Guam
    (B) The Philippines
    (C) Yilan
    (D) Japan

95.What is the main topic of the talk?
(A) How to get free tickets
(B) How to get higher scores in Earth Science
(C) A brief introduction of the park's favorite site
(D) A brief introduction of the National Science Museum

96.Where can tourists get the free tickets?
(A) at The National Science Museum
(B) at the campus
(C) at the Facebook headquarter
(D) at the coffee shop

97.What will suffer if there is an algae bloom?
(A) sediments
(B) living organisms
(C) the land
(D) minerals and nutrients

98.According to the castle owner, which of the following colors are not suited for the photoshoot at the castle?
(A) white
(B) black
(C) gray
(D) yellow

99.Where does this talk most likely take place?
(A) the wedding venue
(B) an ancient castle
(C) a film studio
(D) the speaker's house

100.Who can be the potential candidate allowed to use the castle?
   (A) a student responsible for the festival party
   (B) a professor wanting to know the history of the castle
   (C) a tourist who is an avid castle lover
   (D) a movie director

NOTE

模擬試題 解析

 **PART 4**

聽力原文與中譯

Questions 71-73 refer to the following video

This is ...Jason Thornes...welcome to wildlife Kitchen...apparently, I have competition...so one of the inhabitants is going to use traditional kitchen ware...and I have the delivered cooking utensils...let's take a look...grill pan...it's new but it seems a bit overshadowed by the villager's flagstone...I've gas so that makes me quicker to finish a table of ten...I also have a whisk and a food processor...that makes me more efficient...they are still using knife to chop the large slice of beef...I'm gonna put the beef into the food processor...it's done in a few seconds...great...oh dear...the producer brings me a new refrigerator...is it necessary? I've got to say that the whisk is amazing...the camera should really take a close-up...though villagers are experienced chefs using rolling pins....my dough is almost done and I'm gonna scatter some scallions...

問題71-73請參閱下列視頻

這是記者...傑森・索恩...歡迎來到野生生物廚房...顯然我已經有了競爭對手了...所以其中一位居民要用傳統的廚具...而我有送至的烹飪廚具...我們來看下吧...方形平底烤鍋...這是新的但是這跟村民的石板相比似乎有點相形見絀...我有瓦斯所以讓我能更快完成一桌十人份的料理...我還有攪拌器和食物處理器...所以這樣讓我看起來更有效率...他們還在用刀子在切大片的牛肉...我要將牛肉放置到食物處理器中...這在幾秒內就完成了...很棒...噢！我的天啊...製作人幫我帶了新型冰箱...這真的有必要嗎？我不得不說這個攪拌器令人感到吃驚...這台相機應該要拍下近距離的...儘管村民們是有經驗的廚師使用著麵棍...我的麵團已經好了，然後我要撒些青蔥了...。

試題中譯與解析	
71. Why does the man say, "a bit overshadowed by"? (A) because he exaggerates the claim (B) because he wants the flagstone as a gift from villagers **(C) because he thinks the flagstone actually prevails the company's expensive products** (D) because now he cannot cook faster	71. 為何男子提到「a bit overshadowed by」? (A) 因為他誇大的宣傳效果 (B) 因為他想要從村民那獲取石板當作禮物 **(C) 因為他認為石板實際上勝過公司價格昂貴的產品** (D) 因為他現在無法烹飪的更快速
72. Why does the man want the camera to have a close-up? (A) to make villagers jealous (B) to impress the producer of the show (C) to give photographers a genuine feel **(D) to highlight and promote the product**	72. 為何男子想要攝相機近距離拍攝呢? (A) 讓村民們感到忌妒 (B) 打動節目的製作人 (C) 給攝影師真實的感受 **(D) 強調並推薦產品**
73. What distinguishes the food processor with villagers' knife? (A) its engine **(B) its efficiency** (C) its price (D) its weight	73. 食物處理器和村民刀子的區隔處在於? (A) 引擎 **(B) 效率** (C) 價格 (D) 體重
答案:71. C 72. D 73. B	

- **第71題**，這題的話，其實男子對於送來的廚具感到振奮也覺得應該會勝過這種不起眼地方的用具，但是看到村民的flagstone卻不免感到相形見絀，才講了這句話（覺得可能用石板烤或煮更勝用廚具或更有風味），所以最可能的答案為**選項C**，廚具的鋒芒被蓋過了。

- **第72題**，男子在講這句話時，是特地要攝影師打了特寫，其實有故意要觀眾看到這個產品，有推銷和廣告的效果在，故答案為**選項D**。（視頻中的廚具均是置入性行銷的產品）

- **第73題**，這題是比較兩樣產品的優缺，the food processor確實在效率上勝過村民的刀子，故答案為**選項B**。

聽力原文與中譯

Questions 74-76 refer to the following video

This is ...Jason Thornes...welcome to wildlife Kitchen...the competition is still on...I'm gonna fry the dough with scallions...hmmm smells good...and the egg...totally forget to mention that I have one of the expensive Chinese woks delivered today...I'm gonna fry water spinach with beef and onions...it can be instantly heated...that makes it highly recommended...would like to have one myself...the villager is now making a traditional soup and stirs with a large ladle...I've got to say that lumber-made ladle is good...I should probably sneak back out there and steal it...kidding...where is my ladle?...it's got to be here somewhere...it's made of metal...kind of ok...what...the producer just told me the price of the ladle...a price that I can barely afford...

問題74-76請參閱下列視頻

這是記者...傑森・索恩...歡迎來到野生生物廚房...競爭仍存在著...我正要煎裹有蔥的麵團...嗯嗯聞起來蠻好的...還有蛋...全然忘記提到我有很昂貴的中國中式炒菜鍋今天送到了...我要先炒空心菜和牛肉跟洋蔥...這個鍋子能夠即刻受熱...如此一來讓其值得高度推薦...自己都想要有一個這樣的鍋子了...村民正製作傳統的湯以大型的長柄勺攪動...我必須要說的是那個木材製的勺子蠻好...我可能應該要偷偷跑到那裡去然後偷走...勺子...開玩笑的...我的長柄勺在哪呢...一定在某處...這是金屬製的勺子...還可以啦...什麼...製作人剛告知我這個勺子的價格...幾乎是我勉強能付的起的價格呀...。

試題中譯與解析	
74. What is being advertised? **(A) the Chinese woks** (B) the dough with scallions (C) fried water spinach (D) the ladle	74. 廣告所宣傳的是什麼? **(A) 中國鐵鑄鍋** (B) 裹著蔥的麵糰 (C) 炒空心菜 (D) 勺子
75. What aspect of the pan does the speaker applaud? (A) the origin (B) the light weight **(C) the heating part** (D) the shipment	75. 鍋子的哪個部份是說話者所讚譽的呢? (A) 起源 (B) 輕盈的體積 **(C) 加熱的部份** (D) 運送
76. Who most likely is the speaker addressing? **(A) housewives** (B) villagers (C) executives of the kitchen wares (D) the producer	76. 說話者最可能在對誰說話? **(A) 家庭主婦** (B) 村民們 (C) 廚具的主管 (D) 製作人
答案:74. A 75. C 76. A	

解析

- **第74題**,打廣告的項目很明顯是Chinese woks,故答案要選**選項A**。
- **第75題**,這題可以對應到對話中的it can be instantly heated,故答案很明顯是**選項C**,加熱的部分。
- **第76題**,這個視頻最有可能的談話對象有很多,不過最有可能的收視觀眾會是家庭主婦,所以有煮菜和相關廚具的主打,故答案要選**選項A**。

聽力原文與中譯

Questions 77-79 refer to the following news report

After a few discussions and further attempts to merger with the largest car company, the result is not fruitful...the company actually has more problems than they are to the eyes of the audiences...the issue remains...if none of the investors is willing to finance...then the company will disintegrate and employees will be jobless.......hold on we have a breaking news...the spokesperson is making an announcement...

Spokesperson: It's sad to say that our CFO of the company transferred the money that is gonna be used to pay the employees and some of it actually came from earlier investors...this actually adds salt to injury...and unfortunately...the CFO is in another country now...

問題77-79請參閱下列新聞報導

在幾次的討論和嘗試性的與最大型的車廠合併後，結果是徒勞無功的...公司實際上比起觀眾們所著眼的部分，有更多的問題存在著...議題仍舊...如果沒有投資客願意資助的話...那麼公司就會瓦解而且員工會失業...等等...我們有新聞快訊...發言人有公告要發佈...

發言人： 令人感到悲傷的是，我們公司的財務長將用於支付員工薪資和有些實際上來自於投資客的金錢轉移了...此舉確實讓問題更為雪上加霜...而不幸的是...財務長現在正位於其他國家...。

試題中譯與解析

77. What can be inferred about the merger? (A) successful (B) fruitful **(C) futile** (D) mysterious	77. 關於併購可以推測出什麼呢？ (A) 成功的 (B) 富有成效的 **(C) 無效的** (D) 神秘的
78. Which of the following is closest in meaning to disintegrate? (A) intact (B) mystify (C) consolidate **(D) dismiss**	78. 下列哪個選項近似於「disintegrate」？ (A) 完整的 (B) 使困惑 (C) 鞏固 **(D) 解散**

79. Why does the spokesperson say, "adds salt to injury"? (A) To salvage the public image of the company (B) to provide proof of the transferred money (C) to refute the information from earlier news report **(D) to show that it makes the situation even worse**	79. 為何發言人提及「adds salt to injury」？ (A) 拯救公司的大眾形象 (B) 提供移轉金錢的證據 (C) 駁斥稍早之前新聞報導的資訊 **(D) 顯示這會讓情況更糟**

答案：77. C 78. D 79. D

 解析

- 第**77**題，試題中提到的merger是not fruitful，所以可以對應到選項的 futile，故要選**選項C**。
- 第**78**題，這題是詢問同義字的部分，所以其實答案是**選項D**。
- 第**79**題，發言人會說這句話的原因是這讓情況更糟了，因為後來注入的資 金又遭到財務長的挪用等，故答案要選**選項D**。

聽力原文與中譯

Questions 80-82 refer to the following news report

Normally, this kind of news only lasts for a week...but it seems that things are going to be more dramatic than we can imagine...in the morning news, the CEO of the company is being put into the custody for insider trading...and the CFO of the company was found dead on a cruise...according to the police report...there wasn't defense wound of any sort...which makes this incident more creepier...is he getting framed and murdered? Is this a conspiracy? Perhaps he didn't take the money and flee the country? there are still many suspicious points that we can only wait for the police to find out...and this is Cindy Chen in London...

問題71-73請參閱下列新聞報導

通常，像這樣的新聞只會維持一週…但是奇怪的是，這似乎比我們想像中的更為戲劇化…在晨間新聞中，公司的執行長因為涉及內線交易而被拘留…而公司的財務長被發現死於航遊客輪上…根據警方的報告…現場沒有任何的防衛性傷害…這使得事件變得更為毛骨悚然…他是被誣陷且謀殺的嗎？這會是個陰謀嗎？或許他不該將錢帶走且逃離國家？而還有許多可疑的疑點，我們只能等待警方找出真相…這是辛蒂‧陳在倫敦的報導。

試題中譯與解析	
80. According to the news report, what is the CEO getting accused of? (A) forgery (B) murder **(C) insider trading** (D) corruption	80. 根據新聞報導，執行長被控告什麼罪名？ (A) 偽造文書 (B) 謀殺 **(C) 內線交易** (D) 貪汙
81. According to the news report, what can be found on a large ship? (A) money (B) illegal documents (C) cruise **(D) corpse**	81. 根據新聞報導，在較大型的船上頭可以發現什麼？ (A) 金錢 (B) 違法文件 (C) 航遊 **(D) 屍體**
82. Where is the news report given? (A) Egypt **(B) Europe** (C) America (D) Asia	82. 新聞是在何處播報的呢？ (A) 埃及 **(B) 歐洲** (C) 美國 (D) 亞洲
答案：80. C 81. D 82. B	

解析

- 第**80**題，這題要注意細節的部分，還有是詢問關於CEO的部分，故要選**選項C**。
- 第**81**題，這題的話試題中的a large ship要對應到cruise，這樣一來就很容易選了，所以可以得知在船上發現的是財務長的屍首，故答案要選**選項D**。
- 第**82**題，這題的話最後結尾記者有說道自己所在何處，記者身處的地方是英國，英國包含在歐洲的範疇，故要選擇**選項B**，即歐洲。

聽力原文與中譯

Questions 83-85 refer to the following recording

There is an explosion in the huge warehouse...but it is deduced that this is a result of the mega forest fire...those items in the storehouse are inflammable, paper, wood furniture, and clothes...and the forest fire somehow spurs the growth of fire...we are asking for more assistance...the helicopters are spreading water to halt the increasingly rampant fire...whereas some of the rescue teams use both the chemical powder and water to make the fire smaller...nearby local residents are being forced to leave their houses...and luckily no one was injured...finally here comes a massive rainfall...really like a miracle...but unfortunately some forest animals died...

問題83-85請參閱下列錄製訊息

在這大型的倉庫發生了爆炸...但是可以推論這是大型森林火災的結果...那些項目在倉庫中是易燃的，紙、木製傢俱和衣服...而森林火災有點促成了火勢的成長...我們要求更多的支援...直升機正灑水來暫緩日益蔓延的火勢...而有些救援團隊同時使用了化學粉末和水讓火勢變得更小...鄰近的當地居民被迫要離開他們的房子...而幸運的是，沒有人受傷...最終來了場豪大雨...真的像是奇蹟一般...但是不幸的是，有些森林動物死亡了...。

83. Which of the following items is not instantly-lit in the fire accident? (A) inflammable items (B) furniture **(C) plastics** (D) clothes	83. 下列哪個項目在火災意外中不是易燃品? (A) 易燃的品項 (B) 傢俱 **(C) 塑膠** (D) 服飾
84. What is mentioned about the firefighters? (A) they are able to tackle the explosion (B) they are forced to leave the house **(C) they demand more help** (D) they don't have the authority to use helicopters	84. 關於消防隊員的部分何者正確? (A) 他們能夠處理爆炸事件 (B) 他們被迫離開居住的房子 **(C) 他們要求更多的幫助** (D) 他們沒有權力使用直升機
85. Which of the following was ravaged by the forest fire? **(A) beasts** (B) helicopters (C) firefighters (D) local inhabitants	85. 下列哪一項受到森林大火的肆虐? **(A) 野獸** (B) 直升機 (C) 消防隊員們 (D) 當地居民
答案：83. C 84. C 85. A	

解析

- **第83題**，試題是詢問not instantly-lit，故可以排除掉inflammable的所有項目，選項出題也沒有照著列，還是可以先排除掉大範疇的inflammable items, furniture, clothes，故答案為**選項C**。
- **第84題**，視頻中沒有提到消防隊員能應付爆炸的部分等等，最主要的部分是他們需要幫助，這對應到聽力原文中的we are asking for more assistance以及選項C的內容，故答案為**選項C**。
- **第85題**，這題的話要看到最後unfortunately some forest animals died，animals等同於beasts故答案要選**選項A**，也要注意前面聽到的物品或項目就是了。

聽力原文與中譯

Questions 86-88 refer to the following advertisement

Best Jewelry is having an exhibition in the coming Fall...the tickets are harder to get than usual...because international celebrities will be attending the event...all tickets are sold out in a day...which makes the hosting company profitable...there are four types of jewelry that will be exhibited...diamonds, gold, sapphires, and pearls....and they have never been exhibited...of course there are interpreters on the scene...all of them are actually multi-lingual, can converse several languages at the same time...don't worry that if you have a spouse that is not a local here...and you are probably wondering whether the resold tickets on other websites are authentic...it's not false...you might get the profit of selling them to others...grab the chance...

問題86-88請參閱下列廣告

倍斯特珠寶在即將來臨的秋天要舉辦展覽...門票比起以往更是一票難求...因為國際名人都會參加這個活動...所有的門票都在一天內銷售一空了...這也讓主辦公司獲利...一共有四個類型的珠寶即將要展示出...鑽石、黃金、藍寶石和珍珠...它們都未曾被展示過。當然，現場會有口譯員在...實際上，他們所有人都懂數國的語言，能夠同時以幾種語言進行交談...別擔心如果你的配偶不是當地人...而且你可能也會想，在其他網站上重新銷售的票是真實的...不是仿冒的...你可能可以藉由銷售票給其他人而獲利...抓住機會吧...。

86. What is unique about the Best Jewelry at the exhibition?	86. 在展覽會場中，倍斯特珠寶的獨特處為何？
(A) its comparatively low price	(A) 價格相對低廉
(B) its durability	(B) 耐用性
(C) its design	(C) 設計
(D) its debut	**(D) 首映**
87. Why does the speaker mention "don't worry that if you have a spouse that is not a local here"?	87. 為何說話者提到「don't worry that if you have a spouse that is not a local here」？
(A) to enhance the authenticity of the jewelry	(A) 提高珠寶的真實性
(B) to demonstrate the credibility of the company	(B) 彰顯公司的信用度
(C) to clear the doubts	**(C) 清除疑慮**
(D) to make sure everyone will get the ticket	(D) 確保每個人都會拿到票
88. Which of the following will not be showcased in the approaching exhibition?	88. 下列哪一項不會於接下來的展覽會中展示出呢？
(A) silver	**(A) 銀飾**
(B) gold	(B) 金子
(C) pearls	(C) 珍珠
(D) blue-like gems	(D) 藍色般的寶石
答案：86. D 87. C 88. A	

解析

- 第86題，這題要小心些，因為沒有一開始就提到這部分，而是到了中段才提到they have never been exhibited...這其實是要說明展示會會是珠寶首次亮相，故要選**選項D**。
- 第87題，說話者會講這句話是因為展示會其實有設想到這點，所以有準備口譯員，故可以不用擔心這部分，但題目中沒有提到這點，而是用較隱晦的方式表達，其實也是澄清一下疑慮，這樣購票人就不會因為一些考量而不購買了，故答案要選**選項C**。
- 第88題，這題是詢問不會展示的部分，其實沒有提到silver故答案要選**選項A**，另外要注意的是藍寶石sapphires換成了blue-like gems。

聽力原文與中譯

Questions 89-91 refer to the following news report

Six months have passed since we launched the news...time truly flies....and I'm the reporter ...and of course there are other reporters...let's see who is here also...those sitting near the giant glass wall...they are interpreters and...there are a few waiters walking around serving wine and mini-burgers...I'm loving the chicken wings...but they haven't been served yet...and there are plates of candy apple...I'm gonna taste that for you...finally lots of people waiting outside at the entrance....and where are the those celebrities...I see...they are in the auditorium...listening to music...and those curtains are about to be removed...wow...the dazzling jewelry...just too striking...

問題89-91請參閱下列新聞報導

自從我們新聞發佈到現在已經過了六個月...時光真的飛逝...而我是新聞記者...而當然還有其他的記者們...讓我們來看看誰也到這兒了...那些坐在靠近大型玻璃...他們是口譯員和...這裡有幾個服務生四處走動服務酒和微型漢堡...我喜愛雞翅...但是還未上菜...還有幾盤糖霜蘋果...我來替你嚐嚐...最後許多人都在入口處等候著...還有那些名人們...我懂了...他們在講堂裡...聽音樂...而那些簾子正要移除了...哇！眩人奪目的珠寶...真的太耀眼了...。

試題中譯與解析

89. Where most likely are the listeners? (A) at an annual auction **(B) at the precious metal exhibition** (C) at the jewelry processing plant (D) at the interpreter training center	89. 聽眾們最有可能在何處? (A) 在年度銷售會 **(B) 在珍貴金屬的展示會** (C) 在珠寶加工廠 (D) 在口譯員的訓練中心
90. Which of the following could be about to be served? (A) mini-burgers **(B) chicken-wings** (C) candy apple (D) wine	90. 下列哪樣料理正要上菜? (A) 微型漢堡 **(B) 雞翅** (C) 糖霜蘋果 (D) 酒
91. What field does the speaker work in? (A) jewelry design (B) cuisine catering (C) music industry **(D) journalism**	91. 說話者最有可能在哪裡工作呢? (A) 珠寶設計 (B) 佳餚外燴 (C) 音樂產業 **(D) 新聞業**

答案:89. B 90. B 91. D

解析

· **第89題**,從聽力段落中可以得知是珠寶展,聽眾是在珠寶展示會,珠寶換成了precious metal故答案為**選項B**。

· **第90題**,其餘三個選項都端出了,僅有雞翅是還未上菜的,故答案為**選項B**。

· **第91題**,可以推斷出說話者是記者,記者是新聞產業,故答案要選**選項D**。

聽力原文與中譯

Questions 92-94 refer to the following weather report

This is news anchor Bella James...good afternoon...it's been quite tranquil...outside...the clear view and clouds and altocumuluses...don't seem to show up in the sky...but a typhoon is about to approach...and let our weather man tell you the weather in the following week...

Weather man:...thanks Bella...the typhoon tripled its size near Guam...and we are predicting three different routes...first...it's gonna land on the Philippines...and then move towards the southern parts of the Taiwan...the second route is...it will first hit Yilan and make its landing...and move north towards Japan...the third prediction is that it will be the largest in history and set its foot on Japan...then sail towards Korea, the predictions of other international news coincide with our second route...

問題92-94請參閱下列天氣預報

這是新聞主播貝拉‧詹姆士...下午好...外頭...一直相當的寧靜...晴朗的景色...雲和高積雲在天空中似乎都看不見...但是颱風正接近中...讓我們的天氣員告訴你接下來一週的天氣狀況...。

天氣播報員：謝謝貝拉...颱風將會在靠近關島時以三倍的體積增大...而我們預測了三個不同的路徑...首先...它會在菲律賓登陸...而然後移至南台灣...第二個路徑是...它會先襲擊宜蘭並且在宜蘭登陸...之後北移至日本...第三個預測是，颱風會是史上最大的且在日本登陸...然後駛向韓國，其他的國際性新聞的預測與我們所預測的第二個路徑吻合...。

試題中譯與解析

92. What can be inferred about the weather before the typhoon? (A) cloudy and with different types of clouds **(B) clear** (C) windy (D) rainy	92. 颱風來之前，可以推測出天氣是如何呢？ (A) 多雲且有各式不同的雲體 **(B) 晴朗的** (C) 風大的 (D) 下雨的

93. According to the weather man, where did the typhoon gather the most strength? (A) at Korea (B) at Japan **(C) at Guam** (D) at the Philippines	93. 根據天氣播報員, 颱風於何處獲取最大的力量? (A) 在韓國 (B) 在日本 **(C) 在關島** (D) 在菲律賓
94. If the prediction of the typhoon goes as the international news, where will the typhoon first strike? (A) Guam (B) The Philippines **(C) Yilan** (D) Japan	94. 如果颱風預測路徑跟國際性新聞吻合的話，那麼颱風會首先襲擊哪裡? (A) 關島 (B) 菲律賓 **(C) 宜蘭** (D) 日本

答案：92. B 93. C 94. C

解析

- **第92題**，聽力段落中提到了晴朗無雲且有高積雲，所以要選**選項B**，clear。
- **第93題**，天氣播報員提到...thanks Bella...the typhoon tripled its size near Guam...，故答案要選**選項C**。
- **第94題**，這題是詢問颱風的預測路徑，如果預測跟國際預測路徑一樣的話，颱風首先會攻擊的哪裡，而在聽力結尾敘述出現prediction of other international news coincides with our second route...，所以找到第二路徑時颱風首先襲擊或登陸的地點是哪裡就是答案，所以可以得知答案為**選項C**。

聽力原文與中譯

Questions 95-97 refer to the following talk

This is Mark Wang......and I'm so pleased to introduce you to the design near our park...it's vivid...and thousands of tourists take pictures with lively volcanoes and the model of the formation of the lake...but they often forget that uploading the photo to the Facebook will get free tickets of the National Science Museum...which are attainable at our coffee shop...I'm sure some of you learned those during high-school...first...the rainfall washes away several minerals and nutrients on land and these things are sedimented into the lake...which make the algae bloom...the oxygen is deprived from the algae which make the fish and other living organisms harder to live...eventually all species die and more sediments are washed into the lake making the lake smaller...eventually it has become the land...this is called the formation of the lake...

問題95-97請參閱下列談話

這是馬克・王......我對於要向你們介紹我們公園的設計感到開心...這是生動的...數以千計的觀光客都會跟活現的火山和湖泊形成的模型拍照...，但是他們通常都忘記，上傳照片到臉書上能獲取國家科博館的免費門票，而門票在我們咖啡店可以拿到...我確信你們之中有些人在高中時學習過這個了...首先降雨從陸地上沖刷了一些礦物質和營養素，而那些物質沉積到湖泊裡頭...讓藻類繁盛...氧氣被藻類剝奪了，此舉讓魚和其他活生生的有機物更難生存了...最後所有物種死亡，而更多的沉積物沖刷到湖泊裡頭，讓湖泊更小了...最終成了陸地...這就是所謂湖泊的形成...。

試題中譯與解析

95. What is the main topic of the talk?
(A) How to get free tickets
(B) How to get higher scores in Earth Science
(C) A brief introduction of the park's favorite site
(D) A brief introduction of the National Science Museum

95. 此篇談話的主題為何？
(A) 如何得到免費的門票
(B) 如何在地球科學科目上獲得更高分數
(C) 公園最受喜愛景點的簡介
(D) 國家科博館的簡介

96. Where can tourists get the free tickets? (A) at The National Science Museum (B) at the campus (C) at the Facebook headquarter **(D) at the coffee shop**	96. 觀光客於何處可以獲取免費的門票? (A) 在國家科博館 (B) 在校園裡 (C) 在臉書總部 **(D) 在咖啡店**
97. What will suffer if there is an algae bloom? (A) sediments **(B) living organisms** (C) the land (D) minerals and nutrients	97. 如果藻類繁盛的話,什麼會受到影響? (A) 沉積物 **(B) 具生命的有機體** (C) 陸地 (D) 礦物質和營養物質

答案:95. C 96. D 97. B

解析

· **第95題**,這題的話其實是公園最受喜愛地點的簡述,故答案為**選項C**。

· **第96題**,聽力段落中有提到which are attainable at our coffee shop,故答案要選**選項D**。

· **第97題**,這題仔細聽的話可以得知答案就是**選項B** living organisms,其會因為藻類的繁盛而影響。

聽力原文與中譯

Questions 98-100 refer to the following live show

We're lucky enough to invite the castle owner...and he is not here to talk about the castle...but about the wedding...welcome...James...

James: you probably wonder how many people are having a wedding photoshoot at our castle...I've got to tell you fewer than ten...so using your fingers you can count that...you can see what's on the slide...really enigmatic...right...there are some effects of the fog...make it even more illusional...I highly recommend white, black, gray wedding dress...but not purple and yellow...and we're not renting it for educational purposes or Halloween parties...or opening it for tourists...but we really can use it for films...horror films or thrillers...that someone is chasing after you...

問題98-100請參閱下列現場節目

我們很幸運能邀請城堡的擁有者...而他來此不是來談論城堡的...而是談關於婚宴...歡迎...詹姆士...。

詹姆士： 你可能會想有多少的婚宴在我們的城堡中拍照過...我必須要告訴你少於10個...所以用手指頭就能數的出來了...你可以看到簡報圖...真的神祕...對的...有些霧的效果...讓這看起來更錯覺的...我高度推薦白色、黑色、灰色婚宴服飾...但不是紫色和黃色...而我們不將場地租借用於教育目的或是萬聖節派對...或是開放給觀光客們...但是我們真的可以將其用於電影...恐怖片或驚悚片...那種有人在你後面追著你的...。

試題中譯與解析

98. According to the castle owner, which of the following colors are not suited for the photoshoot at the castle? (A) white (B) black (C) gray **(D) yellow**	98. 根據城堡主人，下列哪一個顏色不適合於城堡拍攝？ (A) 白色 (B) 黑色 (C) 灰色 **(D) 黃色**

99. Where does this talk most likely take place?	99. 此篇談話最有可能發生在何處?
(A) the wedding venue	(A) 婚宴場地
(B) an ancient castle	(B) 一棟古代城堡
(C) a film studio	**(C) 攝影棚**
(D) the speaker's house	(D) 說話者的家裡
100. Who can be the potential candidate allowed to use the castle?	100. 誰可能是能允許使用城堡的潛在人選?
(A) a student responsible for the festival party	(A) 負責節慶派對的學生
(B) a professor wanting to know the history of the castle	(B) 想要知道城堡歷史的教授
(C) a tourist who is an avid castle lover	(C) 極度愛好城堡的觀光客
(D) a movie director	**(D) 電影導演**

答案：98. D 99. C 100. D

解析

· **第98題**，男子有提到幾個顏色適合，也有提到不適合的，可以直接用刪去法，故答案為**選項D**。

· **第99題**，地點的話最有可能的是在攝影棚，故答案為**選項C**。

· **第100題**，這題要看到結尾but we really can use it for films...horror films or thrillers，所以僅可能租借給電影公司，故答案要選跟電影公司相關的人或接洽談租城堡者，最有可能的是**選項D**。

NOTE

國家圖書館出版品預行編目(CIP)資料

新制多益聽力題庫：短獨白,附詳盡解析. 2/
Amanda Chou著. -- 初版. -- 新北市：
倍斯特出版事業有限公司, 2021.01　面；公分.
-- (考用英語系列；29)
ISBN 978-986-98079-9-9(平裝附光碟片)
1.多益測驗

805.1895　　　　　　　　　　　　109021105

考用英語系列　029

新制多益聽力題庫：短獨白2，附詳盡解析（MP3）

初　　版　　2021年1月
定　　價　　新台幣420元

作　　者　　Amanda Chou
出　　版　　倍斯特出版事業有限公司
發 行 人　　周瑞德
電　　話　　886-2-8245-6905
傳　　真　　886-2-2245-6398
地　　址　　23558 新北市中和區立業路83巷7號4樓
E - m a i l　　best.books.service@gmail.com
官　　網　　www.bestbookstw.com
總 編 輯　　齊心瑀
特約編輯　　陳韋佑
封面構成　　高鍾琪
內頁構成　　菩薩蠻數位文化有限公司
印　　製　　大亞彩色印刷製版股份有限公司

港澳地區總經銷　　泛華發行代理有限公司
地　　址　　香港新界將軍澳工業邨駿昌街7號2樓
電　　話　　852-2798-2323
傳　　真　　852-3181-3973

Simply Learning, Simply Best!

Simply Learning, Simply Best!

Simply Learning, Simply Best!

Simply Learning, Simply Best!